THE CULL

RESOLUTION PENDING

GARY CARTER

Population

G J Carter

One foot in the future one foot in the past
We stop in the now and still move with a task
The right and the left feet always take turns
They leave the past for future concerns

The shadows we leave disappear with our passing
But our seeds should continue they seem everlasting
We maintain and sustain but always complain
As humans we grow but this growth leaves a stain

Eventually good things must come to an end
Our size was demise too late for a mend
The fat lady sang when we spent our last penny
In the now it seems, we are eight billion too many

PROLOGUE

Wanderers

The gift of life was eternity's flower

It lasted a brief and finite hour

If life was the pollen, the scent and the seed

Then intelligent reason gave it beauty and deed

G J Carter

I am Arnold Bask and I have a tale to tell, I was both a protagonist and an antagonist in this saga. I lost some good friends along the way, not that they are dead now, or ever will be, the MUZE seen to that. At the age of 36 I embarked on a device that would take me on a wandering outside of space-time. Thankfully, I still had that youthful mind and toughness that would help me fall in love and survive, despite the alien MUZE within my being.

I was a 1980's child, when wearing singlets and thongs to the local mall or beach was the norm, especially with long and hot summers. Australian speech was simple: 'G'day mate' and 'see ya', were standards. Suburban Summer Hill in Sydney was a wonderful place to live, with perfect weather all year round. Friends and fights were on every corner. The eighties decade was a time of economic splurge, Rubik's cubes, and Space Shuttles. It was also when I learnt to defend myself at the local Police Boys Club. My ancestry dated back to the village of Borup in Denmark, a place that produced tough Vikings. Those were the days of population balance and dying before your thirtieth birthday, in childbirth, or by a sword through your liver. I also needed to be tough, Summer Hill Vikings had a diverse range of cultures and gangs to contend with. Street smarts and life skills were other words from my teenage world, and I had my fair share of both. I graduated at Sydney University, with distinctions, in the profession of Electrical Engineering, which Vikings would never have dreamed of. I never thought in my twilight years that I would be living on a mountain farm with an ocean lapping at the doorstep.

This tale will take you away from reality and open your eyes to a probable future. A story that started back on the African savannah with an upright Australopithecine Lucy making her way from the trees to the coast. She was a hunter gatherer, the first wanderer. Humans love to wander and wonder. Our real human development problems did not start until the 1850s with the industrial revolution, when planet wandering took the people and trade to all the recently discovered lands. The human population from that point went ballistic. Pandemics and wars helped delay the inevitable, but nobody took any interest in the growth problems. Our heroes beat the villains in wars. Religious faith in a better life after death convinced millions that God was all caring.

American appliances, capitalist greed, new drugs, and industrialised food production brought all the new age wanderers fictional happiness. Today we continue to populate, to our own detriment. Let me now take you back to the days of sea adventures, just before the Industrial revolution. A time where this story begins and where humans were intent on a whale and seal slaughter, that would nearly cull their great populations to extinction.

For Science, speculation and prescience.

Cosmos 2021 - 'Seeing is believing and humans long to see things.'

CHAPTER ONE

Connections

J ob Gaffer Jackson's name, like many ex-convicts from Tasmania was an alias. He was born Jack Jobson and at the age of fourteen he was sentenced to seven years in the colony of New South Wales. His crime was acquiring two free apples on the ground under a vender's wagon. The vendor and the law did not see the story that way and within six months Jack was on his way to the Great Southern land. Because he felt he had been treated so badly by the court, he became bitter and angry. The result was in 1833, after an altercation with a guard, he ended up at the notorious Port Arthur prison in Van Diemen's

Land.

The Governor on this future Apple Isle, was Sir George Arthur. George was a religious zealot who would give a well-behaved convict a chance if he obeyed the overseer's order, and God. He replaced harsh physical punishment with punishment of the mind, and reformed Port Arthur's convicts through a regime of religious instruction and worship. Ship building and other trade skills were introduced on a large scale at Port Arthur. This provided selected convicts with useful education that they could take with them when freedom was offered. Jack saw this as a way out, and a chance to get a life skill. A little bit of religion would not kill him either. He became one of Arthurs well behaved and subsequently received his ticket of leave. Jacks ship building skills bought him into contact with the Whaling industry and a job fraught with danger.

In the 1830s, the revenue from whale exports was greater than any other produce from Van Diemen's Land, it was the backbone of Hobart's economy. Jack joined a crew of men braving the Southern Ocean in a ship called Noahs Respite. He signed on with an alias, Job Jackson, a breakaway from his forgettable past. Long voyages were needed to capture Sperm whales. They would set off from the ships in tiny wooden boats to pursue these enormous animals. The whale numbers were so vast that their carcasses would clog the Derwent River. On one occasion Job returned to

Hobart in the company of a flotilla of boats. They had so many carcases you could walk across the Derwent on the backs of the whales without getting your feet wet.

After several more months at sea, Job returned to Hobart, it had been his third outing after signing up. He walked from the wharf to the Hope and Anchor Inn, passing the whale oil lights on the city's streets. The job of a sperm-whaler in the deep ocean was dangerous work, he was tied, and he wanted a change. As he walked into the bar the stench of sweat and rum hit him like a wave. To an outsider the smell of dead whale blubber would have overridden all. Whale men were oblivious to their own odour. He sat with a friendly lad named Amos, a whaler and sealer from a land base operation. He told Job that catching Right whales was a better option, it could be done from land bases. Amos gave Job an introduction to Captain John Booth of the Sea Empress. He liked Jobs experiences and signed him up. The ship worked out of Hobart, for Job it was to be a painful adventure. Right whales were plentiful, along the east coast and at one stage there were thirty-five stations in Van Diemen's Land alone.

The next day they sailed north towards the Freycinet Peninsular. From the deck of the Sea Empress Job could see the Wineglass Bay whaling station. He pointed out to Amos the change in water colour from deep blue to red:

'It's Right whale blood Job, and that's why they call it a wine glass bay, and by the way, those black spots you can see are shark fins, big ones, tigers and whites mostly.'

It was that moment the Captain Booth called:
'Right prey off the starboard bow!'
The crew sprang into action.

They lowered three boats, with crews of three and headed towards their beast. Being the new crew member, the captain accompanied Amos and Job on their boat. Job was managing the lines, methods differed on this ship and Job was learning on the run. Amos was one of the three on harpoon duty. He cast it into the flank of the gentle beast, the other two went for eyes and heart, none were kill-shots. An unexpected flick of the whale's tail hit the boat, as the whale dived, Jobs line looped and snagged his left wrist. Job was airborne and hit the water screaming. Seconds later he surfaced in a pool of blood and with a jagged splinter of bone where his hand once was. The captain grabbed onto Job's clothing and dragged him over the gunnels of the boat with seconds to spare from the jaws of a three metre Tiger Shark. Amos slipped off his belt and applied a tourniquet to Job's left arm to stem the bleeding. The whale surfaced dead in the water and the captain yelled to secure the catch. He swapped places with another crew member and went back to his ship. He then gave orders for Amos to row to shore and have the wound tendered to. Because Right whales were plentiful in these waters, the death rate among whalers was huge. Job was lucky.

On shore they had a medical tent, the doctor was also the barber and dentist. He called himself Dr David Russell, but his qualification had some doubt attached, he also looked after the stock. The good news was he knew how to cauterize the wound. Job was kept in the tent for several days in case of infection. He was attended to by an Aboriginal girl called Mary Local. Her clan was known as the Toorernomairremener from the Oyster Bay tribe. Local was a far easier last name. Mary was a pretty girl about 16 years old, Job loved her care and company. Over the week they became close. He was healing well. Dr Russell provided him with a large steel fishhook, two shaped timber pieces and some heavy-duty kangaroo leather strapping. He showed Job how to fashion a workable prosthetic for when he was fully healed.

Dr Russell was watching the way Job and Mary were interacting. He had a kind heart and knew Mary's life story was full of trauma. Job had been recuperating for two weeks when Captain Booth of the Sea Empress rowed ashore. He was of two minds when he saw Job's condition, leave him here or offer him a ride to another destination. Job was of no more use on a whale boat. He sat with him and explained the options. Job said that he preferred to leave. Captain Booth told him that they would not be going back to Hobart, but seal hunting from Port Phillip to Kangaroo Island. Hobart and the East coast were becoming overcrowded with whalers, and he had decided to try his luck with seals, a trade that was just as lucrative.

At this stage, Dr Russell stated that Job still required some care, and he had no problem if Mary accompanied Job. At first the captain was reluctant, but when he saw the three smiling faces, he realised Job and Mary wanted to be together. After discussion he said he would drop them off at Hog Bay on Kangaroo Island. As he departed Wineglass Bay, Job felt a strange connection to the place. He pictured a time when the bay was blue, the sand white and not covered in blood. He wondered if it would ever return to that state of peace. He had no idea that a descendant named Marlin Jackson would think along the same lines.

Job and Mary were on the ship for a month helping where they could. Job was now fitted out with the hook prosthesis and was becoming a real talent at gaffing the day's fish catch, for the kitchen. The crew were good at nick names, and it was not long before Job was being called Gaffer, the name stuck, as did his fishing skills. Job, due to his remarkable survival had taken to reading the Bible and the Teachings from Port Arthur had re moulded his faith. Captain Booth was also a devout religious man and as ship captain he married Mary and Job on board. They parted company at Hog Bay and bid farewell to the crew and his good friend Amos. Captain Booth introduced Job as Gaffer to and old fishing friend, who said with a laugh:

'With a hook like that, Gaffer has a place on my boat as long as he doesn't try to shake my hand.'

Kangaroo Island was a seal and wallaby fur haven for the ex-convicts who escaped Tasmania. Many of these wild men had taken Aboriginal women and they etched out a good living in the fur trade. The other expanding industry was fishing, and Gaffer was built for it. Mary would be happy too, some of the Aboriginal girls were from her Oyster Bay tribe. Many were ill-treated by the wild men, and she could help them when possible.

Hog Bay was where Mary and Gaffer decided to settle down and start a family. The new family name had washed away the convict stain and the whaler's stench, Gaffer Jackson was now a fisherman. He had seen the light, through survival on the killing fields of whale and seal carcasses. He had found his empathy in witnessing the wanton savagery and treatment of native women. He had had enough and needed peace. The Port Arthur indoctrination and struggles had made Gaffer a deeply religious man. With courage and perseverance, he would succeed. His connection to this great southern land was now set in concrete.

Gaffer's family grew in an area once known for its pig population, Hog Bay. Later, it would be renamed Penneshaw. They became a family of fishermen.

Eventually Gaffer and Mary built a home overlooking the bay. It had a large front window and they often sat looking out at the seasonal changes, the stars at night and lightning strikes from storms at sea. They felt touched by nature and named their children after natural events. Their first child was a girl called Sunshine. She was followed by a boy called Cyclone. It was a long-standing family tradition that went on for generations. So, it was no surprise when Cyclone named his son Starlight in 1890, and in 1920 Starlight Jackson named his son Moonbeam. Gaffer and Mary settled in well, they had a good life, with eight children in total.

Sadly, Mary died giving birth to her last child, Gaffer called her Tempest. He missed his Mary. As he aged, he would often sit on their lounge looking out from their large window thinking of her. That window was a metaphor to his life. At night when the stars in his Heaven shone, Gaffer looked out the window as if it were a tunnel into time. He could plan the future and think back to the past.

CHAPTER TWO

Time warp anomality

In the summer of 1950 in the small coastal village of Emu Bay, on Kangaroo Island, off the Australian southern coast, an auction was taking place. This was not a normal auction it was a special land release of a fertile evergreen acre that the Jackson family had always been keen to purchase from the Government. It was going under the hammer and would sell for a song. Moony Jackson knew this as he made the first bid. Being the only one at the auction he got a bargain. To say this piece of real estate was a special family acquisition was an understatement, especially when you had the knowledge of its history. This history related to a story that was handed down in the Jackson family Bible.

To an outsider the land at Emu Bay offered a good ocean view from a high vantage point and the opportunity to build a wonderful weekend cottage for a sea change escape. To Moonbeam it had a more mystic appeal. An historic incident and message received on this tiny patch of verdant green had a story that challenged your knowledge and place in the scheme of things. That message was found by Moonbeams great grandfather Gaffer Jackson who had always fished in these waters.

In the centre of that verdant acre at ten minutes to midnight on the 15th of July in the year 1852, the Jackson family of fishermen were gathered around a fire listening to Gaffer Jackson read from the Bible. It was a clear star-filled sky of wonder and bared testament to Gaffer's belief in creation. His son Cyclone and the crew of other family members listened intently to a verse from Proverbs, Gaffer knew it off by heart and quoted:

'But the wisdom that comes from heaven is first pure; then peace-loving, considerate, submissive, full of mercy and good fruit, impartial and sincere'.

Gaffer stared into that page with the Bible open on a blanket by his feet. The onlookers vision suddenly focused on the page as it began to glow purple. A strange jelly like oval-shaped object, the size of a Duck egg materialised and glowed with warmth. The men looked on with astonishment, it was a sign from God. After it cooled, Gaffer held it in his good hand, it felt like holding a de-shelled soft-boiled egg. It then began to warm again, and went hard with a message appearing on its side, the words were:

'ΩβΣπμ-00100201 MUZE-directive Earth languages Anglo—Error confirmed per host, correction required due to time warp anomaly. Instructional request: Bury information object on site and await further contact in precisely one hundred of your years.'

A startled Gaffer looked around at his sons, they were all wide eyed, and Cyclone asked:

'Is that a message from God?'

'It must be son, the wisdom that comes from heaven is first pure'.

The Jacksons were such a God-fearing family at the time, they did what they were told. Gaffer grabbed a solid timber tackle box, tipped out the contents, Cyclone wrapped the egg in a piece of flannel and placed it in the box. He then secured the lid with candle wax. They buried the box under a cairn of rocks, adjacent to a blue gum sapling and offered up a prayer to the Lord. Gaffer then read from the Gospel of Luke about Peter the Fisherman. Their net had been cast; the family had dealt with the mystery in a Godly manner. They then went about their business and the fishing was great that season. The incident was never made public. Gaffer wrote about the mysterious event and the return date in the family bible, and it was passed on over the generations.

Moonbeam Jackson grew up in Penneshaw and at the age of twenty went off to serve his country. His World War Two experience was not exceptional, he had a bit of the Jackson luck. He served in the RAAF as a radio operator and gained some experience in the first months of the war in New Guinea. New Guinea was followed by a deployment to Airforce operations in Darwin just prior to the bombings in 1942. He was off duty when the first bombs dropped. He was at the Victoria Hotel in Smith Street. This pub, which survived the bombs was the local watering hole for a lot of the servicemen in town.

Much of Moonbeam's time in Darwin was spent on radio repairs and clean-up work around town. It was at the Victoria Pub that he met his future wife Ruth, she was a nurse. At wars end they took up the offer of farming land in Parndana on Kangaroo Island. The Australian government had instituted a Soldier Settlement Scheme, providing returned servicemen and their families with twelve hundred acres of land to farm. The town of Parndana was established as a hub for a new farming community. His father was still in the fishing game, but Moonbeam wanted a change and farming had appeal.

In 1950, three years after Moonbeam and Ruth had started their farm at Parndana on Kangaroo Island, Moonbeam was informed of his duty by his father and given funds to purchase the land at Emu Bay. Moonbeam was a gregarious character and well-liked by his mates at the Queenscliff Pub in Kingscote. He often told of the family's alien close encounter story over a few beers. Nobody ever believed it, it just blended with the other embellished tales around town.

On the 15th of July 1946, Moonbeam and his wife Ruth became the proud parents of a son. It was an incredible coincidence, being the same date as the message from Gaffer's God. Ruth was a touch super-stitious and believed, because of the coincidental date, he must be a special boy. They decided to go against tradition in the naming of their first born. Naming children after nature's wonders, although unique, was past its time. It wouldn't be until the 1970's, before there was a resurgence of names like Sunshine and Sky. The Jacksons were fishermen, so, after some de-liberation and negotiation, the idea of naming a child after a fish, found appeal. This idea did not work so well with fish called flathead, mullet, or schnap-per. However, there were fish with more harmonious names, such as Sole, Bream and even Marlin. After a short period of time Ruth and Moonbeam both settled on Marlin, a powerful surface swimmer who would al-ways put up a hard fight. They knew in their hearts that in time their son would become a person of merit, perhaps even a doctor. Moonbeam turned to Ruth with a proud smile:

'I can hear it now Ruth, Doctor Marlin Job Jackson, it's got a bit of a ring to it, don't you think.'

Marlin would grow into an extremely smart boy, as he was very inquisitive. He was destined for a great future. It turned out that he was a prodigy, not in Medicine but in Mathematics and Physics. His parents often wondered where he got the talent from as they thought of themselves as just an average family.

By 1952, a holiday shack had been built on the family acre at Emu Bay. Ruth and three generations of Jacksons were staying at the shack to celebrate two major events. As it was the 15th of July, one was Marlin's 6th birthday, and the other after a one-hundred-year wait, the buried box and egg mystery was about to unfold. The night sky was clear, and the air was crisp. Just before midnight all the Jacksons gathered around the weathered cairn of rocks, at the base of a large blue gum tree. The cairn of rocks was not hard to find, the blue gum tree was now a giant, over one hundred years old and it was still only a third of its potential age. Grandpa Starlight, his son Moonbeam and young Marlin sat with different thoughts. Marlin was only six years old, but his anticipation grew, and he glowed with wonderment. His dad had been telling him of this adventure from an early age. He was a smart boy, he conversed like an adult and even offered suggestions about the possible reasons for the object. This came from his fascination of science fiction books and his well-advanced knowledge of basic science.

A soft breeze swept in from the Southern Ocean as Starlight, after removing the rocks, dug the ground, he quickly tired, and Moonbeam took over. He was frantically digging away when suddenly he heard a thud, the shovel had hit the box in which their ancestor Job Gaffer Jackson had placed the object. Marlin was wide eyed with excitement as he looked on. His grandpa took the box and used a pen knife to scratch out the candle wax that his grandfather had used to secure the lid. It was two minutes to midnight on Starlight's watch, as he unwrapped the egg, from the now rotten flannel. He held the metallic egg high in his hand and shouted: 'Glory be! It wasn't a myth'.

The egg was extremely cold. Marlin begged his grandpa for him to hold it. Starlight could see the boy's keenness and agreed. Moonbeam was not so sure, he told him to drop it if anything strange happened. Marlin held on to it with both hands and the egg began to warm up. The family were no longer as religious as they had been in the past. Grandpa still went to church on Sundays, but Moonbeam and his family were more agnostic these days. This adventure was more of a myth or a discovery of the unknown than a message from heaven. As Grandpa's watch hit midnight the egg started to glow, and all their faces lit up. A message then appeared on the side of the egg. Marlin read the words out as they all stood there in shock:

'$\Omega\beta\Sigma\pi\mu$-001002012 - MUZE-directive Earth languages Anglo, – Instructional request: Marlin Jackson you have been selected as being capable of future direct contact. Treasure this object, studies in math and physics will help you achieve great outcomes. We will be back in contact in phase with your learning and knowledge growth'.

Puzzlement and a strange disappointment engulfed the group. Starlight quipped:

'We waited one hundred years for that!'

Moonbeam was more circumspect, and questioned:

'Where is the thing talking from?'

Young Marlin was objective and asked:

'How does it know my name?'

CHAPTER THREE

To learn is to earn

Marlin began his education at the Parndana Campus. It was a tiny school of about one hundred students, it catered from Pre School to High School. It did not take long for the small staff of teachers to realise that they had an extremely gifted student in Marlin. On his twelfth birthday, the family were holidaying at the Emu Bay cottage. Moonbeam had overseen the alien gift up to that point. It was time for Marlin to take responsibility. Around a campfire, adjacent to that old blue gum tree where they received the gift, Moonbeam presented his son with a specially designed leather-bound box. The alien egg was cradled internally and was secure. The box was fitted with a combination lock. Moonbeam stressed the need to always keep it close, and whenever he could not achieve that, to have it locked in a safe or left with a close family member:

'You have been selected by an unknown entity son; Grandad would have you believe it was from God. I'm not sure if that's correct, or where this will lead you in life Marlin, but you were selected for a reason. Remember to treasure it, and use whatever information it presents to you, with wisdom and careful consideration of outcomes. Do you understand what I mean?'

'Thanks Dad, I will treasure this gift, and I promise you that I will use any information I am given, with humanities wellbeing as the priority.'

Marlin's education was then fast tracked. By 1960 he was the youngest student ever to enter a Head-start programme at the University of Adelaide. His higher math skills had him on track for a Rhodes scholarship. The family farm, at this stage, was diversifying into various products like olives, eucalyptus oil and wine. Agribusiness on Kangaroo Island was very lucrative, so covering Marlin's education expenses was not a problem.

At the age of 18 Marlin followed in the footsteps of the great Stephen Hawking, who was four years his senior. He was accepted into Oxford University where he graduated with first class honours in 1967. He moved to Cambridge University where he conducted post graduate work at the Institute of Physics. It was world renowned for developments in Quantum research, with great minds like Max Born, Dave Dirac and Roger Penrose as guiding lights. Marlin's thoughts and papers on Loop Quantum Gravity and the merging of the four forces of nature, received some scepticism. He was very secretive with his math and only released speculative ideas.

During these formative years at Cambridge University, Marlin shared a student room in Corfield Court at St Johns College. His roommate was David Doyle, he was the son of a wealthy Scottish Industrialist. David was enrolled in an Engineering post graduate course. They became close friends and talked at length on the future and the possibilities of their work. They were both energetic and fit from the regular University rowing competitions. The wins were always celebrated at the Eagle Inn, where they could take their minds off physics for a moment and mingle with Biologists and Natural History people. It was a place where Watson and Crick worked over lunch on the concept of a double helix DNA. Marlin considered it to be brain boosting therapy.

Marlin was a brilliant mathematician, the chalk boards in his room at St Johns College were always covered in a staggering array of numbers and algebraic expressions. Math without scientific testing of hypothesis was a challenging route in the subatomic world. Whenever Marlin hit a wall in calculation, he was assisted from time to time with mathematical concepts that were well outside his own abilities. The 'Object' that was given to him as a boy, was an egg of enlightenment and seem to know when he needed help. He had a safe fitted in his room, where he kept the secure box with the alien egg. He shared the safe with David. Only once in their years at St Johns College did David question what was in the locked box. Marlin did not lie, he said it was a special keep's sake handed down through generations. David never asked again.

On a weekend trip to Scotland in 1969, just after Neil Armstrong walked on the moon. David introduced Marlin to his father Patrick. He was extremely impressed with some of Marlin's ideas and discoveries. By the end of the 1970s, this smart Kangaroo Island lad was the talk of the town in the Cambridge Math and Physics community. They had at first ignored his ideas and concepts because it was a time where there was an overabundance of theories and hypothesis in quantum math.

American scientists from the 1940s were making huge steps in the development of transistors, integrated circuit boards and then basic IBM computers. This helped them put man on the moon in 1969. In 1982 Commodore Business Machines under the leadership of Jack Tramiel, a former taxi driver, developed the Commodore 64 personal computer. It became the best-selling personal computer of all time. This was just the start, the world-wide-web was just around the corner. Humans would become part of a huge social amoeba, an experiment in mass distraction and a technological revolution.

In 1969 the Cold War was still running with the mutually assured destruction dialogue. President Nixon ordered a squadron of eighteen B-52s loaded with nuclear weapons to race to the border of Soviet airspace to convince the Soviet Union that he was capable of anything to end the Vietnam War, that the Soviets were financing. The USSR was in the first throws of devolution. At this time, people like Marlin were making great advances in Physics. Cambridge University sadly, had a history of spying for the Soviets.

The room opposite Marlin and David was occupied by another engineering postgraduate student named Boris Podoloff. His parents were separated, his father Yuri was a Russian diplomat at their embassy in London. He became embroiled in a spying saga around the time the 'Cambridge Five' were making headlines in the news again. This followed an MI5 investigation. The Cold War was always hot between London and Moscow. Yuri was sent back to Russia, leaving his wife and son in London. Boris was required to continue his studies. His mother Margaret had a well-paying job and was able to assist Boris with his education fees. Margaret was English and MI5 had no objection to this arrangement. Of cause the family would be kept on a watch list, Boris was a suspect agent. He loved both his parents and often talk to his father in Moscow. Yuri was extremely interested in his son's studies and longed for the day the family could join him in the Great Soviet Republic.

Boris was a bright boy but shy and withdrawn. He did not associate with the other students at the University, he just plodded along with his studies and kept to himself. It was on a cold winter's day in November and just prior to exam season when Boris left his room to stretch his legs. David had just left for a study course in Liverpool. Marlin was working away with algebraic expressions on his chalk board and unaware that David had left the door ajar. He was concentrating so hard on an equation that he did not see Boris standing near the door observing him. It was at this time that the object glowed purple and revealed an algebraic expression that was beyond Marlin's comprehension. Boris was mesmerised by the purple glowing egg, he said nothing. He then saw Marlin read an inscription on the egg and record it on his chalk board. The smile on Marlin's face said it all.

Whoever sent the message, or whatever this object was, it had revealed an answer for Marlin. Boris was puzzled and went back to his room. He knew Marlin was making big strides in the physics and mathematics community and now he realised that he was getting help from somewhere. Yuri had taught Boris that information and knowledge, that was beyond explanation at any time, may be of value in some future time. Boris rang his father that night and told him he had witnessed an unusual event. He did not elaborate; he knew about MI5 monitoring. His father recorded a diary entry to follow up on the unusual event when they met in person. He did nothing more:

'Boris get on with your studies and do not bother with the other students. We will discuss your observations when we next meet. I expect you to excel in your career choice, so make me proud.'

Boris would never forget the incident. He met Marlin in the corridor about a week later and he asked what his interests were. Marlin was amazed, Boris had never said more than two words to his neighbours. He told Boris that he was working on Quantum Gravity equations. Boris just nodded and started to walk off. He stopped suddenly, and turned, he could not resist the urge:

'I saw a purple glow under your room door the other day, what was that all about?'

Marlin just laughed and jokingly said:

'I had aliens visiting from the outer limits.'

Boris was unmoved by the reference to a current American TV show and maintained a dead pan look on his face. Marlin responded in kind with a quickly thought up lie:

'Only joking with you mate! It was just an experimental ultraviolet light with which I was working on. It's for a study my class is undertaking.'

Boris did not believe him but took it on face value and did not bother Marlin again. As time went on Marlin and David and their company dreams blossomed. Boris did not forget. His studies ended that year, and he went home to Moscow. His mother filed for divorce. Yuri had become a person she no longer felt safe around. He now associated with a growing group of nationalist KGB people. They sensed, as Bob Dylan sang:

'The times they are a changing.'

With his father's associates, Boris secured a trainee Engineering position in Vladivostok. He worked hard and climbed through the ranks over the next twenty years, always towing the Communist Party line. Eventually Boris was running the company. The Gorbachev-Yeltsin era then changed everything. The fall of the Soviet Union and reunification of Germany in October 1990 provided great opportunities. The rebuilding of East Germany needed engineers with the skills that Boris now had control of. His connections in the new Russian Republic made Boris a wealthy man and an Oligarch in a new dictatorship.

While the ex- movie star, President Reagan, was planning Star Wars from space in 1980, across the Atlantic, Patrick Doyle was signing his share of the company over to his son David. At the same time, he made Marlin the major shareholder in a new business called Jackson-Doyle enterprises. This company then took out patents on Marlin's designs and concepts, to cover the intellectual property rights. They then built a state-of-the-art complex, like a mini-Silicon-valley in Glasgow's growing industrial hub. It thrived with a range of its own computer programmes and products. Marlin was well on his way to making his first million with his brilliant concepts.

Back in the summer of 1970, David and Marlin were in London having a well-earned break from their studies. Marlin needed some Australian banter, so they found themselves at a crowded party in Earls Court. Across the room, dressed for the heat, in a sky-blue halter neck dress, was an extremely attractive lady. Marlin could hear her voice. It was soft and mellow and obviously Australian. Sally was a teacher from Sydney, she was sadly orphaned when her parents were killed in a car accident. Sally was in London on an exchange programme. Marlin had a shyness when it came to forming relationships, he had a few short flings in his university days, but the business of science and enterprise took up most of his time. He introduced himself with a stumble, a spilt beer on her beautiful dress and said sorry. His next statement was corny and nervous, but to Sally it was cute. He said he had tripped over her beauty.

They had a good chat about the local scene, and Sally promised to show them around the next day. They were all staying at the same hotel, so it was no problem finding her. The place was full of ex-pat Aussies. The down-under birds, as they were referred to as, were all falling for Dave's Scottish accent. Marlin lost Sally in the crowd, but he could not stop thinking about her. He also could not find David. He was last seen chatting to a girl called Monica, from Melbourne. They caught up with Sally at lunch time, on the following day. She took them to 'the Surrey', just off the Strand. It was full of newly arrived Australians. London's Earls Court, or as some called it Kangaroo Valley, was always the mecca for young Australian travellers. In the 1970s it was the only place in London where you could buy an ice-cold beer and socialise with compatriots. It was a party village, where back packers shared rooms, women, and combi-vans.

The décor 'the Surrey' consisted of a couple of boomerangs and some pictures of cricketers on the walls. The smell of smoke, sweat and wet beer mats was overwhelming. It was the sort of place you would find a loud-mouth Bazza Mackenzie, they felt rather uncomfortable. There were handshakes of welcome and bawdy songs and far too much noise. They had one pint of home-brewed lager and decided to have lunch elsewhere. It was at the Zambesi Club, when Marlin realised, he had fallen in love at first site, it was mutual. Sally talked all afternoon, Marlin was smitten. They did not even notice when David disappeared, mumbling something about Monica. As it turned out, both young men met their future life partners at the same place, and function. It was a future talking point.

Sally and Marlin fell in love the minute their eyes met, but it was another four years before they returned home. The wedding was held in Parndana. They honeymooned at the cottage at Emu Bay, and that is where Marlin told his new wife about the 'Object' from another realm. He swore her to secrecy. There were only four people now who knew about the 'Object', his father and mother being the other two. At this stage he had not even told his best mate David about it. Plans for a future travel concept were on his mind, and when the time was right David, as the project engineer will have to be informed.

The newly-weds lived at Parndana for a while. Marlin had several trips, back and forth to Scotland before they brought a property in Adelaide. It was in Glenelg, looking south towards his family home on Kangaroo Island. Marlin needed to have access to international travel for work and to be close to relatives. In 1978 they decided it was time to start a family. Their first born, a baby girl they named Sole, was a smiling bundle of joy.

Life in the Jackson household was full on and happy. In time their second child was born, another girl they named Bream, and their house became a home. They often holidayed at Emu Bay and had their fair share of overseas trips. Sally was kept busy organising Marlins travel and running around after the kids. She was also back to teaching at a local school. Marlin's business was growing exponentially, his success bought him good contacts, and to a lesser extent, envious enemies.

David Doyle was now running all the engineering and development projects that their companies had in Scotland and Australia. They met regularly, and both maintained their close family ties. Marlin had discussed the 'Object Project' plans with David and both men were excited about the new venture.

Around the time that Einstein was developing his theory of relativity, two other lesser-known physicists were experimenting and making mathematical suppositions of their own. They were Nikola Tesla and a colleague of Einstein named Burkhard Heim. Their respective fields covered a gamut of ideas on Gravity and Magnetic field theory. In the 1970s, using the previous ideas and studying the new fields of electro-gravitics and electro-kinetics. Marlin made some astounding breakthroughs in the math surrounding Loop Quantum Gravity.

Over the next twenty years, Jackson-Doyle enterprises developed and patented more devices. Marlin's ideas were revolutionizing main frame computers by utilising quantum coding. Other industry competitors were intrigued by the security and complicated math behind these devices. Computer speed and particle physics was the new frontier and Marlin was the driving force. Within a few short years his personal

wealth was in the billions. He was still strongly involved in the development and study of unified field
theory. He also invested heavily in the National Particle Accelerator centre at the CERN Institute. In 2011
at the age of sixty-five, Marlin Jackson was in the top
ten of Forbes list of world billionaires.

CHAPTER FOUR

The 'Object Project'

Marlin's last offering to the scientific community, just prior to stepping down from various academic position, was to name his new corporation the 'Object Project'. This left some of his peers and acquaintances pondering his intentions. He had gathered around him a dedicated team of project specialists. This included David Doyle his university friend and business partner. David ran all the engineering aspects of the project. The teams first design meeting was held at the Hobart office. David's drawings of the 'Object' at first confused the specialists. They were puzzled why there was a need for the egg shape design. David turned to Marlin, who was behind the physics and math of the concept. Marlin knew that the alien egg shape was an essential part of the transfer ability, but he would not disclose the other world reason, instead he spoke of its special geometry and symmetries:

'An egg has an elliptical form, with two focal points, and it is a very symmetrical object. The rotational axis of symmetry and its cone like geometry make it the perfect vehicle for space-time travel. Our dough-nut or torus electro-magnetic coils are fitted in symmetry to the surfaces of our vehicle. This makes for a smooth transition of eddy currents and a reduction in hysteresis losses. At this point on a subatomic level loops of gravitons will resonate with strings of elec-tro-magnetic bosons, and if my calculations are cor-rect, it will allow our device to traverse space-time.'

Dr Robert Smith, Chief Scientist, and Control Room Manager, made the only comments:

'Much of that has been tried before Marlin, without transitions. What formulations have differed in your models?'

'Good question Robert, I came across some calcula-tion expressions that led to the inclusion of certain resonant ripple frequency changes in the design plan, which balanced out my equations.'

Marlin spoke with such conviction and with no con-cept of failure, that the group took his words on face value, and just nodded in agreement.

The plans now were for a move to Freycinet Peninsu-lar, on the East coast of Tasmania. The company had set up a preliminary office at Coles Bay. Sally remained at home in Glenelg and visited him from time to time at his new retreat. Sole and Bream were both now in their thirties and both had successful careers ahead.

With Marlins wealth, came contacts within the top echelons of Australian society. He had made friendships with Commonwealth Ministers, and in Tasmania the current Premier Mark Thompson was a close confident. Thompson was an avid environmentalist from the Greens party, and he had a particular interest in Marlin's project. Projects like this could lead to more environment friendly energy sources. That was paramount if the world was going to succeed in combating climate change. Tasmania was well ahead of the rest of the continent in relation to its green energy, having an abundant supply of hydropower.

The Freycinet Peninsular National Park in Tasmania was an ideal place for this project. It offered calm waters, security, and a solid granite seabed, that was a necessity in the science of matter transfer. Marlin's influence and money secured the uninhabited Refuge Island in the Great Oyster Bay. The Tasmania Parks and Wildlife Service was the government body responsible for protected areas of Tasmania on public land, such as National parks. They were convinced by Marlin's large future fund donation. The fact that this was only a short-term lease with full reparations. The deal was done, and the work began.

This also included permission to build a more extensive access road and a new private wharf at the end of Malunna Road, on the southern end of Coles Bay, which would not impede hikers on the Peninsular or Hazzard walking track. This idea had the locals impressed as it would be great for future tourist and business expansion when the project was completed. The location was perfect for security as well, it allowed for a natural bush barrier from prying eyes along the Hazzard trail to the Isthmus trail, which was another access point to Wineglass Bay. Hikers and campers could still make their way to the southern end of the peninsular. Hazzard beach would have a clear view of Refuge Island, but the project would not be visible from there as it was on the northeast side of the island. The wharf would be fenced off and security gated. As a bonus the Freycinet Lodge went on the market just before the project got underway. Marlin purchased it as an accommodation hub for his staff. It would also make a great future investment prospect.

All the information, approvals, paper trails and emails concerning the 'Object Project' were well secured with commercial protection, with Premier Thompson's blessing. All employees and contractors were required to sign agreements that protected these construction and trade secrets. As far as the public were concerned this was an exploratory drilling rig looking at rare minerals that could be used in battery research. Marlin had employed a marketing genius to keep the enquiring media snoops at bay.

There was to be limited accommodation on Refuge Island, eventually the island would be cleared and restored to its previous condition. In the early days of construction, the blasting noise was a problem to the Tasmania Parks and Wildlife Service, as was the assembly of the rig and projects steel supports. It was a challenge to keep them and the locals happy, as the Freycinet Peninsular was Tasmania's first National Park, and a pristine location. The resident seal population was monitored and appeared unaffected. To accommodate some of the hardware, that came directly from David Doyle's manufacturing plants around Australia, or by container ships from Scotland, two wharfs had to be built. One wharf was on the North side of the Island for equipment unloading, and another at the south end of Coles Bay for human traffic.

By 2016 and known only to Marlin and a few trusted associates at the time the 'Object' was more than a company name, it was a place, a time, and a device. The 'Object' was a 13.5-metre-long, 7-metre-wide, egg-shaped solid iron bullet with a titanium skin. It was supported by a one-way locking lip sitting on the outer steel toroidal coil carrier. This one-way locking lip was a fail-safe because there was always the possibility that the 'Object' could be launched in either direction at exponential speed. The whole project was like a giant solenoid, and it was destined to carry travellers beyond the threshold of spacetime. What his associates did not know was Marlin's family God given inspiration that was laid out on that fateful night in 1952, when Marlin was just a boy. His brilliant mind and a mathematical concept from an unworldly object had kick started his future as a Physicist. It also provided a name for the venture.

The new 'Object' was on a solid rig and platform with the outer steel toroidal coil carrier chained to the granite base of off-shore Refuge Island. The whole structure was suspended over the calm waters of the Great Oyster Bay. In choosing the location Marlin had several criteria. The first and foremost was a ready and reliable supply of cabled in electricity. The Tasmanian energy interests were more than accommodating and discreet in their provision of hydroelectric power and other services, including extreme transformation ratios. Direct current cables were laid from a newly built substation at Swansea, across the bay to Refuge Island. Initially 10x25 megawatt toroidal units were installed for experiments. The artificial intelligence that oversaw the project was a state-of-the-art think-tank called EPACT, which stood for Entangled Particle Algorithmic Computation Technology. It was Marlin's greatest achievement and the reason for the missions need for secrecy. The firewall security was quantum coded and unbreakable. Governments around the world were now taking an interest and empowering agents to monitor the 'Object Project' development.

In earlier experiments primates were used. Sometimes, these poor primates failed to return, and several of the monkeys returned with serious injuries, or died in grotesque manners. These results were strangely like those of the Philadelphia incident conspiracy theories. In 1943 on the East Coast of the USA, German submarines were ravaging shipping. An experiment took place on the USS Engstrom in Philadelphia. Scientists thought that by generating powerful electromagnetic fields on board ships it would render them undetectable or invisible to magnetically fused undersea mines and torpedoes. The process was called degaussing. The story of the 'Philadelphia Experiment' was listed as a conspiracy theory or a hoax. These accounts may have influenced future physicists to ponder the use of magnetic fields on a quantum level. Marlin's breakthroughs were a follow on from those early developments.

The human volunteer mission specialists for the 'Object Project' were tagged as Obernauts. Arnold Bask was one such specialist in the program, a born leader, he knew how to prioritise in any given situation. Marlin had selected him as mission leader from their first interview in the summer of 2017. Arnold had the perfect background in and was across all the developments that came out of Jackson-Doyle industries.

He, like all the Obernauts could also be trusted to

keep all information from the 'Object Project' to themselves. They were aware that outside parties and governments would seek to undermine the project and steal Marlin's perfected scientific accomplishments if they could.

All the Obernauts in the program had a science background and degrees in differing disciplines, they were specialists. They were all brave men who knew what they were getting into. Jim Hunter was a hero in waiting and had a zero-fear-factor rating. He was an ex-SAS commander and an extreme sports fanatic, so it was no surprise that he was first to put his hand up for mission one. Like Arnold Bask, Nick Peabody and Christian Taylor, Jim had no strong family ties. It was a condition that Marlin insisted on, the unknowns in this project could lead to sacrifice.

They all went through psyche evaluations and a two-year training programme to sharpen their skills in the operational science behind the 'Object'. Although the EPACT computer artificial intelligence was the main project control mechanism, the men needed to know emergency procedures and operation strategies. The effect on their biological make up was the greatest unknown. Unlike artificial intelligence, humans can think in abstract, and a mission such as this would need that ability.

The program had a successful outcome with a mission in early 2018. A macaque monkey named Jewells returned with no visible side effects. Due to this success Marlin and the team decided it was time to send a human, naturally Obernaut Jim Hunter was first to put his hand up. They had a great send off at the lodge for Jim in early February. Then the launch on 28 February 2019 went well. Everything seemed to go as per plan, but on return the 'Object' capsule was empty. Jim was classed as a non-return and the team was devastated. All EPACT could report on was a statement:

'Insufficient capacity, Obernaut Hunter evacuated per unknown interference.'

The video and audio from internal recordings were also deleted. EPACTs answer to this was: 'Insufficient capacity in algorithmic processes.'

Over the following months, all the data was subjected to vigorous scrutiny and no faults could be found. Jim's disappearance was a mystery. Speculation was that the 'Object' was scanned by forces unknown, and that these forces had somehow dematerialised Jim. We were all saddened by his disappearance. The memorial service and wake were held at the Freycinet lodge near the platform. He was saluted with honour, the life of a good friend now gone but never forgotten. Some of the video footage of his life as an extreme sportsman made some of the small gathering cringe. A brass plaque was placed on a rock overlooking Wineglass Bay as a tribute to Jim.

CHAPTER FIVE

Pandemic predilection

The Covid-19 outbreak and pandemic, plus the bush fires from Christmas 2019, put the whole 'Object' program on hold for months. Marlin was now preoccupied with another major problem. His aging parents Ruth and Moonbeam were in a Senior's home in Parndana, and the western half of Kangaroo Island was facing unprecedented summer bushfires. The fire started on the northwest coast from lightning strikes and burnt out of control. The whole island, including the Flinders Chase National Park, was now under threat. Marlin was concerned that his parents were unsafe and wanted to move them to the holiday cottage at Emu Bay, which was out of the danger zone and close to the ocean. He then went back to the Parndana farm to assist the farm manager in preparations for evacuation. As it turned out the fires did not reach them, and their farm was saved.

These events impacted Kangaroo Island as well as other parts of Australia, in the 2019 summer from hell. The aftermath of this tragedy saw thousands of square kilometres burnt out in many parts of Australia. Climate change had made such an impact, that the bushfire smoke could be seen from space. People were killed and homes were destroyed, the wildlife suffered the most. The National parks were turned to cinders, littering the landscape with millions of animal corpses of birds, reptiles, and marsupials. In the end there was only a black brooding silence of misery, and then, Covid-19 struck, with a force so strong that the entire world would feel it.

The first cases of a viral pneumonia from an unknown cause, were reported in China by Wuhan officials in December 2019. The World Health Organisation or W.H.O, released its first disease outbreak reports about these cases in the following January. The pathogen was confirmed as a 'novel corona virus.' Then China reported its first death and Thailand the first case outside China, it was a human-to-human transmission. W.H.O officially declared it in March as a Covid-19 Pandemic, and everything went crazy.

Australia, to a certain extent, was luckier than the rest of the world. Lockdown restrictions were progressively implemented by the government to restrict citizens movements and reduce their opportunities to gather with other people outside their household. International and national border control measures for some states and territories were introduced. Implementation of physical distancing rules and Australia's borders to all non-residents were closed. All of this played havoc with the 'Objects' programme.

After the bushfire problem settled, Marlin went back to Freycinet, and Sally joined him for a few days. To Marlin it seemed time had caught up with everyone. His parents were just hanging on to the remnants of life, and he and Sally were now in their twilight years as well. The project was paramount, he had achieved a lot in his life, and now, just when success was within his grasp, world events and problems were mounting. He went to the safe in his office to check for any fresh alien messages. He stopped for a moment and pondered the combination lock on the box. He was thinking about the current pandemic and the time he selected the code for his lock. He was still at Parndana, and the class was studying the English history of the Bubonic Plague. He chose the year 1666, when the great fire of London helped solve the problem. He had a cold thought, his studies were reaching a zenith and the world was in lockdown, he hoped it was not an omen.

Because of the pandemic, spying and associated covert plans of world agents, became only a second consideration. There were, however, some players who were always monitoring and watching. The USA was retracting from the world at large. They had a new

President who had the support of the disenfranchised populous. These people were now led by a fear system and a former TV star billionaire who cynically promoted the wealth divide. He did this via social media, rallies, and propaganda. He encouraged race hate and job envy. He denied that Covid-19 was a serious problem, even with a death toll of half a million people. In Russia, the supreme commander and President was content to let a dying superpower rest in peace. His new ally was China. Russia's future fortunes would be swept along in the wake of this new world order, already China and Russia were planning space missions and a base on the Moon.

In the early part of the new millennia Boris Podoloff was well entrenched with the hierarchy of the Kremlin. He was an oligarch of some note, and his engineering businesses were worth millions. His father Yuri had died suddenly from a heart condition in 1999, just prior to the start of the new Millennium. Shortly after the funeral, Boris was going through his father's personal details. Yuri had kept explicit entries in his diaries of people he could trust, and his many enemies. Boris found one entry that bought an instant memory. After Boris had returned to Russia, he had told Yuri all about the way Marlin Jackson had gained information from that mysterious glowing egg. Yuri was sceptical at first but investigated using his diplomatic contacts. Boris was in the business of making money, he had more critical issues at hand. Marlin Jackson and strange glowing eggs was secondary.

It was twenty years later, and the world was in turmoil with Covid-19, Boris's business was suffering as a result. He was once again reading Yuri's investigation on Marlin's earlier developments. A quick Google check informed Boris that Jackson Doyle Enterprises were making huge in-roads in the science of quantum computing and other high-tech gadgets. Boris recalled the glowing egg moment and it reminded him that something was amiss. There was a definite connection between Marlin's great wealth and that communicating egg. It was something strange and unworldly, and Boris wanted in on it. He discussed the issue with friends in the Kremlin. He also had the ear of the President, who had learnt to trust Boris's instincts. Boris was very convincing on this occasion and the President ordered SVR, the Russian Foreign Intelligence Service, to conduct some spying on the Jackson Doyle group. In the first instance three agents were dispatched, two went on a submarine mission to the east coast of Tasmania. The third agent, Sasha Fedovski, was sent to the Russian embassy in Canberra. He was given diplomatic immunity and had free rein to investigate the Jackson-Doyle Industries background and trace the source that fed the communicating egg.

The Yuri Dolgorukiy, Russia's Borei-class SSBN Nuclear submarine, was unaffected by the Covid-19 ravaging Moscow. Captain Sergei Plisowsky' was a 'Gold Star Soviet' and a comrade of the old KGB. The new Russian SVR was just its clone. He had received orders from Moscow to head to Magadan, a Sea of Okhotsk port in the North Pacific. They stated he was to pick up and escort two agents on a fact-finding mission to Australia's east coast and that they had the details. He was informed that the Kremlin was now on a heightened alert, that an Australian oligarch was initiating some sort of plot to undermine their strong Russian economy. All details of this mission were top secret, and he was to send all reports directly to Boris Podoloff via the SVR.

Arnold sat in his room on a chilly April evening sipping on a good Cabernet Sauvignon, he was still thinking about the wake, and the loss of his work mate Jim. He was listening to some Van Morrison music: 'Days like these', the lyrics lifted him a little. When he looked out the window and saw a beautiful sunset over Great Oyster Bay, he realised he had the best room in the resort. Its large window offered a 180-degree view, and the twinkling water reflections of the Bay had a calming effect. Arnold smelt steaks cooking on the balcony below and hunger had an overriding effect on his emotions. The cook Steve Clarke was preparing the night's meal. Arnold could taste the steak in the air. Clarkey did not like to be called just a cook, he preferred the title of Chef-de-Mission, he always said that he was no short order cook, he was a professional. In some ways he was right, he always provided great meals for the staff. Arnold finished his wine, turned off the stereo, and wandered out for dinner, he was in a slightly better mood, tomorrow he would go for a hike before work, it was time to get a bit of nature back into his life and thoughts.

The SSBN Nuclear submarine surfaced briefly, three kilometres off the pristine beach of Wineglass Bay. Two agents from the SVR, Russia's Foreign Intelligence Service, wearing full I-dry wet suits, headed to the beach propelled along by two hi-tech Sea-bob units. They stripped down to their Australian fashion civies, unpacked their limited supply of camping, and hiking gear and buried their scuba gear in the sand adjacent to a well-defined drooping she-oak. Dimitri and Maxim knew their trade well and they both spoke fluent English. Their mission was to gather information on the Refuge Island complex. Satellite reconnaissance had revealed the unusual construct off the Island. This was initiated after reports of magnetic flux disturbances from the area that were playing havoc with their submarine missions in the Pacific. The late April air had a chill to it as they climbed the rise on the approach path to the bay. The plan was to appear as back-packer tourists out for a hike to the southern end of the peninsular. Both men were astounded by the beauty of the surrounding, the view to the south revealed the crimson and green hues of the southern Aurora Australis, it was magnificent. They were pleased with the mission so far. They discussed their surveillance plans and rested till sunrise.

In a back office of the Department of Home Affairs in Canberra, there is a door with the acronym D.O.N.T, followed by a full description the 'Department of National Threats'. Most of the personnel who walked past this door had no interest in the activities beyond it. The operatives of D.O.N.T are solely responsible to the Minister of Home Affairs. Rachelle Castles was one of the agents from this office. She was recently given a task to monitor Dr Marlin Jackson's activities, in association with the development on Refuge Island Tasmania. Rachelle Castles was well trained and experienced for the task, she had come direct from a commander unit within the Department of Defence, having served in three tours of the Middle East. She had also completed two degrees at A.N.U, a Master of Strategic Studies, and degree in Terrorism and Security. At 35 years of age, she was the complete package, 175 cm tall, lithe, and nimble, what some men from a pre 'Me-Too' feminist agenda world, would call a real head turner.

As far as the department were aware, the development at Refuge Island, was just what the Tasmanian

Public Service had stipulated, that is, a mining operation for rare earth minerals. The reason Rachelle
was put on the case was in relation to a Pine Gap
memorandum about the possible signature of a Russian Nuclear Submarine off the Tasmanian East coast.
Another memorandum came through from the Australian Communications and Media Authority about
infrequent magnetic interference with communications in the Great Oyster Bay area of Tasmania. These
two issues sparked an interest within D.O.N.T. Dr Marlin Jackson's movements were now on their watch list.

As dawn broke over the Bay, Arnold awoke to April's
chill. His day was planned, there was a schedule for
a training session on Refuge Island at 11:30 AM, so
rather than take the direct route he decided to walk
the Wineglass Bay circuit to the Hazzard isthmus and
back via Fleurieu Point. Arnold had all morning to
enjoy a hike, so he could just take his time and take in
the ambiance of nature. As he approached the boul-
ders on the clifftop, which overlooked Wineglass Bay,
he noticed signs of an overnight camp just off the
trail, this was strange, as most of the hikers stayed
in the cabins or the campsite adjacent to Honeymoon
Bay. The view from this point was breathtaking, the
pristine surrounds of the Bay attracted people from
all over the world. Arnold could see a school of dol-
phins riding the ocean swell, he also spotted two early
morning hikers sitting on the white sand near the

start of the Isthmus trail off the beach.

He wondered if these two were from the camp he just noticed. Arnold caught up with the two fellows just at the start of the trail, they seemed well equipped for their journey.

G'day he called: 'Great day for a hike!'

Dimitri responded in broken English: 'Good morning'.

'These blokes definitely looked like back-packers, probably Russians', thought Arnold.

This was not strange, many people from Europe walked this trail. Dimitri introduced himself and Maxim, and very quickly warmed to Arnolds friendly nature. Dimitri's mate seemed a bit distant and came across with disinterest.

'Are you hiking to the peninsula end?' asked Dimitri.

'No, I'm taking the Hazzard trail today, back to the Bay, I have a work commitment at lunch'.

'Who would want to work in a beautiful place like this?'

At first Arnold was reluctant to respond, but then he thought, a couple of backpackers would not have much interest in a mining operation.

'Oh, you're right, but a job is a necessity, I work on an island just off Hazzard Beach'.

Maxim then spoke for the first time, in a dry and direct manner:

'And what sort of work do you do Comrade'.

'It's a mining operation and I'm an Electrician', lied Arnold.

The word Comrade raised Arnold's attention: 'These blokes may not be who they seem to be', he thought to himself, so he changed track in the conversation:

'Where are you fellows from'?

'Leningrad, we are having a year off to see the world. It's quite a secluded place you have here'.

'Yes, I find that sometimes the things you do for a living are just where you want them to be.'

'You are lucky to live and work in such a place', responded Maxim.

Arnold ended the conversation: 'Have a good day, this is my turn here, it leads to the Hazard beach trail. Enjoy the hike and watch out for snakes.'

Dimitri and Maxim continued to head south along the beach, all the time looking at the stranger walking away. Arnold was just out of site when they stopped.

Arnold cleared security at the Wharf and mentioned his encounter with the Russians. The head of security was an ex-AIF Commander named James Brennen, he logged Arnold's encounter, and although not overly concerned, made some enquiries with a Border Force mate at Hobart Airport.

Arnold attended the training session, where they discussed upgrades. Because of Jim's demise, a decision was made to strengthen the 'Object' structure and upgrade EPACT. Two additional 25-megawatt units were added. Along with increased structural supports, new nanotech coatings of cross link polymers were applied to the inner walls. The 'Object' itself contained no windows, however it did have 360-degree multi spectrum cameras and a plethora of onboard smart technology senses. An additional duplicated life support system was also installed. All of this was now controlled by EPACTs artificial intelligence, its subatomic chips with encoded quantum weirdness principles were upgraded for extreme computer speeds. The exit and entry air lock were now at the rear of the craft and used Spiro graphic self-fusing nano-struts for seal and re-seal after use.

It was not known if an exit would be possible, or if an

Obernaut would fail to exist on exit. However, these volunteers like former explorers and astronauts assessed that the values of scientific knowledge far outweighed their own short lives. Communication with the 'Object's on-board life support and operational systems back to the Refuge Island base station was possible via Entangled Particle Morse or EPM, another Marlin invention. It utilized the quantum weirdness of separated up-quarks and down-quarks and their ability to communicate instantaneously across space-time distances.

Marlin's parents Moony and Ruth, both contracted Covid-19 at the Parndana Nursing Home. Due to their age they both succumbed. Marlin and Sally were unable to say their farewells. It was a heartbreaking time for the family. His parents were pioneers of Kangaroo Island and had survived bush fires and built an industry. They were buried at Parndana and the whole town had turned up to celebrate their lives. Following the funeral Marlin and Sally made the decision to lease the property at Glenelg and move to Tasmania on a permanent basis. They purchased a two-hundred-acre estate and winery at Bream Creek, one hour drive from Hobart. The home was like a palace and there were two other dwellings on the site for guests. Their daughter Sole was still single, and for the time being that is the way she liked it. She had a Law Degree and had just achieved her degree in Political Science.

Premier Thompson was so impressed with her qualifications, she secured a position in his department. Marlin and Sally were so proud of her, she now had a life path career set in concrete.

Bream had finished University with a Business Degree, met Sam, and married straight afterwards; they then had a son they named Jake. This was a step away from Marlin's plans for naming everyone in the family after a fish species. The only thing Jake had in common with a fish now was his mullet haircut. Sadly, and in keeping with the times, Bream and Sam had an amicable divorce. Marlin saw through Bream's façade of: 'it's all ok mate, we just move on', and asked her would she run the winery. Bream and Jake could not say yes quick enough, they were thrilled at the prospect:

'Thank you, dad, I love you so much, you and mum are the greatest, and they even named the suburb after me, how thoughtful', they all laughed with family happiness.

It was a great outcome for the whole family, they would all be in Tasmania. The Kangaroo Island Parndana farm was still profitable and ran by a good manager. They still had Emu Bay for occasional holiday escapes, so the move to Tasmania was the right move at the right time.

Marlin was now running his businesses from the

offices in Hobart, Coles Bay, and from the Refuge Island control room. David Doyle and Marlin had been in discussions about diversifying their industries. The Covid-19 scare had changed much of the focus in world-wide ventures. Both men now felt they could concentrate their interests in one place. David put it in the words of old Scotland, with a laugh:

'Do ya ken, Tassie is just like Scootland anyhoo.'

The move to Tasmania was also a pay-back to Premier Thompson for all his assistance, the Apple Isle would benefit immensely with this new Jackson-Doyle business model.

David went about the task with vigour, he moved his family to Tasmania with a special Covid entry exception, from contacts in Canberra. Glasgow and Sydney productions were wound back. A large factory complex was purchased near Hobart and a new electronic manufacturing centre began. The concepts that Marlin was now working on were centred around nanotech developments. They were well ahead of the rest of the world in quantum computing after the development of their EPACT unit, and now they had synthesised Nanobot technology to work with. DNA structured Nano poly-bricks with built in blueprints for pre-designed structures, was now the future in the creation of joint utility nano-electric devices. Marlin and the MUZE assisted mathematical theorems would create a Quantum revolution.

Marlin was back at Refuge Island when James Brennan presented a report that came back from Border Force on the Russians. It stated, because of Covid-19, the Hobart airport had restricted entry only for VIP's. There had been no foreign Nationals from the Russian Federation and records showed that the last Russians to enter Tasmania were a family of five from Moscow. That was twelve months ago, a further note added that if there were two backpackers from Leningrad, they were possible undocumented immigrants and must be located. Marlin and James were not overly concerned, but as the next launch date was approaching, he told James to go over security protocols:

'Also, David Doyle and his family may be coming out next week for an inspection of the facility. We have some business discussions. Could you get Clarkey to prepare a feast at the lodge on Friday, we have a new venture to celebrate. I'll let you and the staff know the details at the function.'

The report also made its way via the usual channels to D.O.N.T headquarters and the information conveyed directly to Rachelle Castles. Two days later Rachelle arrived on the Freycinet Peninsular. She was directed to go undercover.

She booked a cabin at Honeymoon Bay and that evening Rachelle went for a coffee at the Treehouse Cafe in the Coles Bay shopping precinct. Arnold, fresh out of the two-day training session was also there, it was an immensely popular location for the project staff. D.O.N.T agents were not your Men-in-Black types, they did not wear wrap-around sunglasses and dinner suits. Rachelle walked in dressed in tight blue jeans, a cream skiffy and Nike runners without socks. The men and one lady in the cafe turned heads at the good-looking stranger. Arnold was struck by her beauty, she sat opposite him and ask for an extra hot flat white skinny, they struck up a conversation.

There is a moment sometimes, when two people first meet, it could be the eye contact or maybe a pheromone transfer, but whatever it was, Arnold felt it now. He was the total bachelor type in life, his work and study had kept him single. He did have the odd short-term relationships, from time to time, but nothing to tie him down. That is just the way he liked it. At this moment however, he was mesmerised. They exchanged the normal small talk about the weather and the Covid-19 pandemic. They briefly touched on politics, and the mess the planet was in, but all the talk was superfluous to the eye contact. Arnold introduced himself as an electrician working on a local project. Rachelle said she was an out of work schoolteacher, who was unemployed when COVID struck. Peabody and a couple of other men from the project came across for an introduction, but they faded away after a quick hello, when Arnold gave them his alpha male look.

Rachelle was staring Arnold; she was besotted by his bright blue eyes:

'What does an electrician do in a National Park'?

'I work at the mining project on Refuge Island, just off Hazzard Beach.'

'Oh, what are they mining for?'

'It's really just an exploratory dig, they think there may be some rare earth mineral deposits under the granite. What about you Rachelle, where are you from, and what brings you to this splendid spot?'

'I'm from Launceston, and I like to hike. I was told that Wineglass Bay was a magic spot to see, plus I had to get away from Launceston. I'm sick of this COVID and all the travel restrictions. Do you hike Arnold?

'Yes, on my days off and sometimes before work, it's a magic place to get away from it all.'

'Are there lots of people on the track?'

'Normally yes, but numbers are down now due to COVID. I went for a walk the other day and met a couple of odd fellows. They were Russians from Leningrad. To me they were like a couple of fish out of water'.

Rachelle's interest in Arnold, apart from the physical, just perked up. 'What luck', she thought, 'first point of call, and I meet the guy who put the Russian report through.'

'What do you mean'? she asked.

'I'm not sure, they just didn't seem like your normal hikers'.

'Do you think it's safe to go hiking alone now Arnold?'

Rachelle was now playing the girl alone in the wilderness routine, she did not want any suspicions about her real identity.

'Yes, go for it, but just to be on the safe side leave your phone number with Constable Mick Booth at the local police hut in Muldoon Street. Let him know your plans, he is a good cop, and will have your back if you need any questions answered. Just in case, if for any reason, he is not available, here is my number as well.'

'Smart move', thought Arnold, 'This lovely lady has now got my number too.'

'Gee thanks Arnold, you're a real gentleman, perhaps we could catch up again before I go home?'

'That would be great Rachelle, I'm off shift in a couple of days, give me a call and you can tell me what you think of the Peninsular.'

'Will do, I best be off now the weather looks good for a hike tomorrow.'

As she left, big ears Peabody, walked over with a smirk like the Joker on his face:

'You smoothy Arnie, two cups of coffee and a virtual date, this will get back to the lads.'

'Yeah, you're just jealous Peanut'.

Truth was, this was just what Arnold needed to help with his own feelings, it was a real lift.

CHAPTER SIX

The danger of predators

David Doyle had just arrived back in Hobart when Marlin rang:
'David how was the flight?'

'Pretty good mate, the family and I managed to get a rare flight out of Glasgow. Monica felt bad about it, because we jumped the queue on a bunch of disgruntled Aussies wanting to get home. It's a pity your government can't set up a faster method for these people, tempers are really starting to flare. This Covid-19 is getting worse over there. I sorted out a lot of our Glasgow Company issues, and I should be able to manage the rest from here from now on. I hired a management group to oversee the downsizing and set up the sale of the main assets.'

'That sounds great, what about the staff?

'I signed ten up on new contracts, and they're keen to come down-under to help with the new plans. I kept a skeleton crew on in Glasgow to work through the transition and paid out large redundancies to the rest, there were no sad faces in relation to the money. It was just the usual issues of moving on and ending work relationships. The ten sign-ups are all long-term staff, with vast experience.'

'That's great news Dave, we should have no problem getting long term visas for the staff. Where are you and Monica planning to reside?'

'We have purchased a place at Battery Point, it has its own wharf. I thought I could come to Coles Bay by boat occasionally.'

'That sounds terrific mate, I might join you, when things settle down a bit. By the way, the Premier was ecstatic when he heard our development plans. I was hoping you could get out here to Refuge Island in the next few days. There are a few things I want to discuss before the Object launch. Why don't you pack your bags, bring the family, and come out for the week?'

'We'll be there pronto by car, the boat hasn't arrived yet, but a bit of R&R sounds great.'

'We are organising a pre-launch celebration at the Lodge. Contact James Brennan at the security office for access arrangements.'

'OK then I'll see you on Monday, bye for now.'

Dimitri and Maxim camped out on Hazzard beach for a couple of days. They were watching the boat traffic from the wharf, taking the workers to the north side of Refuge Island. Maxim had a compass that was used to detect the magnetic actions from the island, for a few hours it was normal and pointed to north. At infrequent moments, the compass would spin wildly, then point directly at the Island. Whatever was happening at the project it was not what you would expect from a drilling platform. Dimitri decided he needed to have a closer inspection. They returned to Wineglass Bay and collected one lot of their scuba gear and headed back to Hazzard Beach. Dimitri donned his wet suit, tank, and a water-proof pack full of equipment he might require. The Sea-bob unit did the rest.

Both men had waterproof hi-tech, off-the-grid, short range communicators, with cryptographic protocols. This enabled Dimitri to talk with Maxim, but only from the surface. Dimitri headed off towards the island. The bay was clear and calm. He surfaced on a rocky outcrop called Promise Rock and rested a moment. He was just two hundred metres off Refuge Island, but the rig was just out of sight. He continued to the Island and came ashore in a small bay with an unobstructed view. Dimitri slipped off his mask and was immediately hit with the stench of fish and basking seals. At first glance it looked just like a drilling rig, but the drill casing was a strange egg shape. It had huge cylindrical cabled drum units around it.

He took some photos, sent copies, and conveyed his observation to Maxim:

'This appears to be some type of high-tech experiment Maxim, I'm moving in closer, this is not a drilling rig, it was more like a huge electro-magnet, out'

Dimitri studied the Island. There was a small bay and a rock ledge that ran to a location not more than fifty metres from what he thought might be the site office. He could see no evidence of perimeter security around this office but there were cameras around the other constructions. There were only four structures in total. The strange egg rig, a building adjacent, that was connected by a huge amount of cabling, a sub-station with large transformers and the site office or perhaps sleeping quarters. Dimitri secured his scuba equipment and sea-bob on a ledge adjacent to the bay. With his backpack on, he slowly made his way along the ledge. A fur seal was resting on the same ledge, it took an exception to the intrusion, snarled, and slid ungraciously into the water. Dimitri smiled and thought for a moment about what he had in common with this creature. Its ability to glide through the water, even if his own method was power assisted. He moved on to a position about forty metres from the office building. He froze for an instant. A ferry was just arriving with two men on it. As he watched they left the wharf and made their way up towards the site office. Dimitri kept concealed until they were out of site. He sensed an opportunity to gather more information and he had come prepared. From his backpack he withdrew a mini black compound cross bow, which had an arrow fitted with a high-sensitive wall microphone and a light gauge recoil cable. Good agents do not leave gear behind, surveillance means nobody knows you were there. This voice bug could listen through walls at fifty metres using short range blue tooth.

David and James made their way off the boat and walked up the ramp towards the office. David had not been back here since the send-off for Jim Hunter. As he walked off the ferry onto Refuge Island, he was surprised by the new development surrounding the Object. The additional cabling and coils gave it the appearance of a giant egg dropped into an oversized slinky. He also noted that the perimeter security around the whole island was updated. James informed him:

'The changes were necessary because there was a recent bit of intel about possible foreign prying eyes. We turn it off when staff are on site during the day, but we have people watching and it was easy to spot planes, boats, and swimmers during daylight hours.

David and Marlin greeted each other on the gangplank with their normal and customary hug and high fives. James left them to it and said give me a call when you need a lift back. There was only one other person on the Island at the time. Dr Robert Smith, Marlin's top computer scientist, he greeted them in the control room. To David's shock so did EPACT, with a woman's computer-generated voice. Marlin explained that EPACTs upgrade had included facial and voice recognition for all staff:

'I was thinking of calling her PAT, but the acronym didn't fit. Don't worry Dave she is not 'Hal' from 2001 a Space Odyssey Dave, not yet at least,' laughed Marlin.

Smith showed David around the new developments. Marlin and David then proceeded to the office. It was at this time, Dimitri's arrow hit the wall.

Marlin, grabbed a bottle of Glenfiddich and told David to take a seat:

'I have a tale for you old mate, I should have done this long ago. Over the years that we have known each other, you have witnessed the mathematical concepts and breakthroughs I achieved. In University some of the math I developed led to a dead end, which is quite common in my field. I have to tell you now, that at times when I hit the wall, I had a little outside help.'

'Well, yee have me full attention now', quipped

David, 'but don't tell me ye are a fraud'.

'No mate, ninety percent of the work was mine, but you may find the outside help a little bit left field. It goes back to my childhood and a family quest and mystery. Our Jackson family bible, from the early days on Kangaroo Island, spoke of a strange encounter at Emu Bay. My fishermen ancestors were presented with an Object from an unknown source, which was delivered in error. The Object glowed purple and revealed a message to bury it and return in a hundred years. My folks back then were extremely religious, they thought it was a message from God, and did what they were told. When I was only six, dad, granddad Starlight and I returned to the spot of the burial, it was the exact day one hundred years later. Dad had purchased the land with monies left in the family wills. The family were a bit sceptical about the mystery, but the bible entry was so convincing, they decided to go through with the request. We camped out and waited to midnight. This is where it gets weirder. I recall vividly the minute we opened the old fishing box, which was buried near a tree. The object was egg shaped and rock hard, I held it. It suddenly softened, glowed purple and revealed a message. It had writing on the side, naming me to be the beneficiary of future advice in relation to mathematical concepts. I kept it with me for years through early school and studied hard, but it never changed. Then one day, while at Oxford, I was working with my thesis on 'Gravity Waves' and there was a glow coming from my draw, it revealed an

answer to an algebraic expression I was having diffi-
culty with. Cambridge was no different, it helped me
infrequently.

The mathematics of quantum science is exceedingly
difficult and every time I hit a roadblock this mysterious egg would glow and disclose an addition to my
formula. This is the reason we have made such great
inroads in our industries. I thought this was the time
to tell you as I am not sure what is going to happen
after the launch, because basically this launch is about
discovering where these messages are coming from.
Do not be alarmed, the concept of a new means of
space travel are still there in the science. But there remain many unknowns. As hard as this is to believe I
think only good can come out of it and I'm sorry that I
haven't told you before. David, you don't appear to be
in total shock?'

'It's a funny thing Marlin, when we were at St John's
college at Cambridge, I remember walking into our
room one night and I saw a purple glow, from your
draw. It was there just for a second and disappeared. I
thought to look but knowing your physics group and
their weird ideas and experiments, I chose to ignore
it and ask about it later. I never thought to follow up
on it, we had exams at the time. For what it's worth
I'm glad you didn't tell me back then, I would have had
you committed. This mystery aside, we have done
well out of it, and whatever happens after this launch
we are in this together. We have always been good

mates and I've got no reason to see any difference now. I just hope we don't start an alien invasion. Where do you think the information is coming from?'

'I know it's not from Earth, so it is alien in nature and the way the object appeared from nothing, it must have quantum transposition behind its physics. This time next week I hope to know more.'

'Well, I am definitely hanging around till launch day.'
'One more thing Dave, this is our secret, there are only three people on the planet who know, ok?'

'Mum's the word, now pour me that whiskey.'

Dimitri conveyed the intercepted message in full detail, Maxim had set his communicator to record then relayed it to the Captain Plisowsky' on the submarine. Dimitri was stunned by the information and knew his masters would be pleased. He recoiled the arrow, packed his kit, and made his way back along the ledge. He donned his scuba gear and took one last look at the beautiful surroundings, feeling incredibly happy with himself.

Dimitri's last message was: 'I'm heading back now, out'.

The seals on refuge island were always in danger of

predators. To a great white shark, something black moving at speed, was dinner. Dimitri was an accomplished diver, he had instincts that generally warned of pending danger. He felt that instinct now, as he swam into a bait-fish ball. Nature had always fascinated him, the predators, and the prey, was basic training in the espionage world. He saw himself in the high seat of the food chain in the spying world. He was not that high in the waters around Refuge Island. There was only shock, no pain, and a brief eye widening thought of his children. He bled out in seconds after the four-metre beast dismembered his legs. The Seabob unit smashed into the rocky base of Great Oyster Bay. The clear water turned red, with pieces of wet suit, scuba equipment and shards of bones descending into the depths. The other fish species finished off the tissued remains of this Russian agent.

Rachelle headed out early on her investigation hike, the sun had just risen on a clear blue-sky day. There was the smell of wet eucalypt trees in the air, following a shower during the night. She very rarely carried a weapon but after talking to Arnold, and the fact that he mentioned the Russians, she decided to be a bit cautious. She carried a SIG Sauer P229 pistol and a waste holster that fitted comfortably into the small of her back. She was dressed in loose fitted Columbia shirts and shorts, which helped cover the gun, and she wore an Akubra hat and comfortable walking shoes. In a backpack she carried water, a hike guide, and some light food, she looked the part of an avid hiker. Rachelle started off on the Peninsular track and made her way to the ridge overlooking Wineglass Bay. She stood there motionless for a minute awe struck by its beauty. She knew its history in detail, the claret shaped bay was once blood red from the whale slaughtering trade, giving it its name. A long-nosed potoroo caught her attention, as it scurried for its day-time hiding spot, just as a noisy flock of yellow-tailed black cockatoos flew overhead. From her viewpoint, Rachelle could see a man digging at the base of a tree halfway along the beach. She thought that was an odd thing at this time of the morning.

Maxim was getting worried, there had been no communication from Dimitri for over two hours. He was not sure if he should get his scuba gear, try to find him, or report back to the submarine. The choice was taken from him, he had already conveyed the recorded report from what Dimitri had seen, but his comrade had not returned. Captain Plisowsky' was extremely annoyed and ordered:

'You will return at once! Dimitri's mission must have been compromised. This intrusion onto Australian soil must be concealed at all costs, we will assume he is dead. He has been trained not to be taken alive, he is a good agent. I'm of the mind that something must have happened on the return swim. We will monitor your arrival'

Rachelle kept close to the tree line as she approached. Maxim who was now fitted out for his return to the submarine was unaware of her approach. She stepped out from behind a tree and said in a friendly tone:

'G'day mate, are you going for a dive?'

Maxim stood there stunned, he was not as cool as Dimitri under pressure. Instinct plays a key role in reaction time. Maxim had two options, engage in a friendly chat with this local hiker or get rid of a witness to their intrusion by drowning her at sea. He was still not of a clear mind after the loss of Dimitri, so he chose the latter. He threw the Sea-bob unit at her and followed through with a round-house punch. Rachelle was shocked by this reaction, but her training kicked in, she ducked the punch and although winded by the Sea-bob she managed a short sharp uppercut onto Maxim's chin. This knocked off his goggles and left him shaking his head. With an evil scowl on his face and blood from a tongue bite, dribbling from his lip. He shifted his weight to his left foot and used his right foot to kick Rachelle on the side of the head. She was stunned for a second and tripped backwards, hitting her head on a rock. As she laid there in a blur, Maxim retrieved his gear, started the sea-bob, grabbed Rachelle by the leg and made for the water.

The wet sand was enough to bring some clarity back to Rachelle's mind, she reached for her gun and shot

Maxim in the thigh. He screamed in pain, let go of her leg and dived through a wave. The Sea-bob dragged him for about two kilometres before he bled out. The trail of blood was quickly sensed by a great white shark, that was now quite partial to Russians. There was no pain in the first bite, Maxim was already dead. The riderless Sea-bob was still running when it was picked up by the Submarine sonar.

Rachelle sat there with her shoes soaking in the waves. It took a while for her full composure to come back, but she knew she had been lucky, that Russian had plans to drown her out at sea. She was now thinking about the information that had led to her involvement in this case, the fact that there were two Russian agents meant that one agent had disappeared and either he had gone back to the submarine, or one was still somewhere between Hazzard's beach and the island project. Rachelle made her way back to the cabin. She contacted a D.O.N.T special support crew, they were instructed to conduct a search by boat from Swansea. The area between the Hazzard's beach and the Refuge Island project had to be patrolled to see if any remains or parts of the other Russian could be found, and while there, survey and photograph the whole Refuge Island project.

Rachelle left a message on Arnold's phone:

'Thanks for all your information Arnold, something's come up back at Launceston, would love to catch up again sometime, it was nice to meet you.'

She was now headed back to D.O.N.T HQ to update her superiors. This was not a mining operation and it required further investigation.

CHAPTER SEVEN

Launch or Lunch?

When the three men were chosen for the next mission, no one expected anyone to survive. They may have been right in more ways than they had contemplated. The three chosen Obernauts were sitting around the bar at the lodge, just after their last training session. This was the first opportunity that the three had been able to talk alone, without Marlin's psychologists peering into their minds. Christian Taylor asked a significant question that night. He was a cool guy with a casual wit, so it came as a surprise to Nick Peabody and Arnold when he said, with a wide-eyed fearful stare:

'What if we were no more than farm fodder on the other side?'

Peabody, who had a short and stubby body and a recollection of last week's lamb roast, just looked at him, the thought had obviously never occurred. After a prolonged moment, Arnold tried to ease the situation by suggesting that poor old Christian being all prick and ribs was definitely not food for the Gods. Peabody, stared off to the distance with a bemused look and said:

'So, I guess I'll be the sacrificial lamb eh!'

With this, Arnold suggested they have one last pub crawl around Hobart, before pre-launch week. Family commitments were minimal and had been addressed. The idea was well received at first, but the guys said it was too far. Arnold then suggested they just go for a meal and some drinks at Swansea instead. Clarkey, working in the kitchen overheard the chatter:

'You can forget that, because the boss is throwing a send-off party for you blokes on Friday. Everyone here is getting an invite, except for some security guys. Even Dave Doyle and family are coming, and I think young Jake, Marlin's grandson is coming as well'

That news cheered them up a bit, at least they will go out on a mission in the memories of others. They all loved having the kid around too, he was a bright boy, and they see so few children these days.

'I suppose you will be keen to impress Clarkey', yelled Peabody.

'Why?' Clarkey responded to the bite.

'We all know how you fancy Bream.'

'She probably won't come; she has a winery to run.'

'Well, you would be too busy in the kitchen, for all those cool moves of yours.'

They all had a good laugh, to Clarkey's chagrin. Arnold was next to comment:

'Well, we all need a release, and although our Hobart pub crawl is off, a great feed of seafood from lover boy over there, sounds like a good compromise to me.'

Arnold had a quick thought to invite Rachelle along. Her message did say she would like to catch up again, but he realised that a one-hundred-and-forty-kilometre round trip from Launceston was a big ask. It would be a great night, but sadly Peabody and Christian's last beers.

It was school holiday time and Sally picked up young Jake from the Bream Creek winery. The travel restriction due to the Covid-19 pandemic were being eased a little, so Bream was looking forward to some more tourists at the winery. She loved Jakes company, but it was a bonus of not having to worry about keeping him busy and out of mischief. He was looking forward to talking to the Obernauts and he loved Grandad's science ideas, in a big way. These blokes were like space heroes to Jake, and they all go fishing.

When they arrived at the lodge Steve Clarke was eagerly awaiting. He had a slight disappointed look on his face, when he noticed that Bream was not with them. He realised of cause, that the winery was keeping her busy at this time and he should not get carried away, just because she smiled at him once. He did not share that disappointment with Jake, like the others here, they genuinely loved having him around. Jake was always asking questions and had a very sharp mind. Clarkey and Arnold told the lad that they would take him fishing the next day off the Island. The smile on Jakes face gave them all a lift.

They all met at the wharf in the morning, and James Brennan had security signed them in, and he led the way to the ferry. They always had gear and bait available on the Island jetty, especially for down time between training sessions. They were having a fun time. After an hour of patience and waiting for a bite, Arnold caught a large flathead. Then Clarkey snagged his line for the second time and lost his tackle, it was not his day. Jake hooked something big. The rod near snapped as he reeled it in. They were all hoping it was the biggest fish of the day and looked forward to a feast that night. Jake fought hard to land it and finally something black broke the surface. At first Arnold thought Jake had hooked a seal. Clarkey reached down to grab the catch.

'It was just some rubbish. It looks like a torn piece of black neoprene from a divers suit.'

As he lugged it to the jetty, he felt the remains of a leg bone wrapped in the neoprene. He said nothing, not wanting to upset Jake. He passed the torn leg piece, which had been ripped off a full diving suit, to Arnold. The men hid their horror from Jake. Also embedded in the partial suit remains was a five-centimetre shark tooth.

James Brennan came running over to see what all the commotion was about. Arnold pointed to the Russian Federation markings on the suit, and James took the hint. He removed the tooth, gave it to Arnold and carried the articles to his office. Young Jake did not see the actual remains, so he was not as shocked by the catch as the others. Clarkey caught on to Arnolds side tracking, for Jakes sake, and diverted Jakes interest to the tooth:

'That tooth will be a good neck piece, eh Jake.'

'Yeah, can't wait to show Grandad. Do you think the diver got away?'

'Not sure,' lied Arnold. 'But I think that tooth is off a white pointer shark, it was probably about four-metres long.'

'I don't think I want to go for a swim around here right now.'

'That makes two of us Jake.'

Arnold broke the thoughts, and winked at Clarkey, to change the subject:

'Well, that's enough fishing excitement for today lads, lets head back to the lodge for lunch. At least we have that flathead, and I am sure I have a special recipe. Marlin should be there by now and Jake has a relevant story to tell him.'

James came back to escort the group to the lodge and whispered to Arnold:

'I just called Mick Booth in Coles Bay, and guess what, he has just been promoted to Sergeant. He is like a new man, all serious and professional. He told me he will organise a forensic team to come up from Hobart tomorrow. He said that the Police area command have been informed that the Department of National Threats in Canberra are very keen to know more about the operations here. They want details of any suspicious occurrences. Mick also said, in the meantime the Island is now a crime scene, so, we may have to delay the launch for a few days.'

When they got back to the lodge Peabody and Christian were at the bar talking to Marlin and Sally. Jake ran in and showed them the shark tooth. His excitement was radiant. Clarkey and Jake then went to the kitchen to prepare lunch. Arnold took the opportunity to tell the whole story. Marlin was annoyed at the possible launch delay, but the thought of Russian and Canberra interference bothered him. He then took control:

'The send-off party is still on this Friday, the launch may now have to be pushed back to Wednesday, So, let's not dwell on this too much, we have many things to think about between now and then'.

Just then Jake came running back into the room, Marlin quickly changed the subject:

'As for you young man, how about we go on a hike tomorrow?'

Jake woke early, he was keen for some one-on-one with his Grandad, and met him at the Coles Bay office the next morning:

'What's that on the wall Grandad?'

Jake was pointing at the steel hook and leather strapped timber moulds, mounted on a wall display:

'That is your ancestors left hand prothesis Jake, they called him Gaffer. A whale ripped his hand off back in the1830's, not far from here. As a matter of fact, that's where we are hiking to today, a place called Wineglass Bay.'

An hour later they were sitting on a rock overlooking the pristine blue water and white sand of the Bay. It was a windless day, and the ocean was as flat as a mill pond. Marlin told Jake the story, as it was handed down to him, how the bay, sand, and water, was once red with whale blood and carcases. He was pointing to the south end of the beach:

'This is our connection to history Jake. Down there on the Isthmus, were some huts, where your ancestor, after losing his hand in a battle with a whale, was treated by a doctor of all trades. He fitted that hand-hook you saw this morning. After your ancestor re-cuperated, he left on a whaling ship, with the doctors aboriginal helper Mary. They got married on the ship and were dropped off on Kangaroo Island. That's where I was born several generations later.'

They walked on the sand and skipped stones on the still water and then headed for home. All the while, Jake was asking questions and enjoying himself. Marlin was loving this close encounter with his Grandson, and his families past. This day would become a treasured memory. Jake would be heading home tomorrow, after the pre-launch send-off party, and all the mission specialists were gathering. The mission was now on everyone's mind.

The send-off party was a great night. Jake got to meet all David's family. The children were having a wild time running around the resort. Clarkey had served up a great feast of seafood, and the wine and beer flowed. Thoughts on the launch took a back seat for a while, and everybody enjoyed the atmosphere. Even the send-off speeches were about the mission success and the wealth of information to be gained. The three Obernauts put on heroic fronts, deep down they would have concerns that this might be their last drink, but it did not show. They partied all night and thoroughly enjoyed themselves.

On the final two days before launch, the Obernauts had to stay in the dormitory accommodation on Refuge Island, it was cramped but their thoughts were on the future. Clearance had been received from the forensic team, that their investigation of the recovered body part, was complete. It seemed there may have been an incursion from a foreign power to investigate the operation here. Security had been increased and at this stage the Government in Canberra did not seem to be interested. Marlin had spoken to the Premier and they had the State Water Police carrying out patrols.

Marlin had some guilt about not telling Jim Hunter the full story of the Object. He discussed it with David, and both agreed, that as these men were putting their lives on the line, they deserved to know the story that led to this project. Marlin told them about the Object, and the alien knowledge that had been conveyed to him over the years. All three were courageous in their response to this new information. They all had the same thoughts:

'How could anyone turn down such an invitation,' said Arnold, with Peabody and Christian nodding in agreement.

Marlin and David sat with the men on the twilight of their mission. They all talked about objectives and feelings. Arnold never spoke about it, but he was also thinking a lot about Rachelle. Their training and mental conditioning had been achieved. EPACT had been fed the full medical and mental background of the three Obernauts. The summated matrix of their existence was now in code, and once they were secured in the Object pods, it would be in total control of their life-forces. Even their thoughts were analyzed with probability algorithms. If all went well, and EPACT did not request an exit, all they had to do was lie on their bunks and await an outcome. Perhaps this would be some form of communication or invitation. Marlin stressed that the mission objective was knowledge, and that each man had the responsibility to each other's wellbeing, as well as this objective:

'Remember men this is an advanced alien encounter, as such they have no reason to harm you. They have helped us achieve the ability to visit them, and perhaps to discover a method of space travel, that humans may one day use to visit new worlds across the Galaxy. You three brave souls are heroes to humankind, we wish you well in this endeavor and we thank you.'

Lessons learnt from previous missions had led to several new inclusions. Obernauts were now required to be fully suited in silver Kevlar breathing skins and to remain on their bunks. The term bunk was probably only a seafaring throw back. They were clear unbreakable polycarbonate shells, which when activated could hold the crew in a state of neutral flux, and hopefully keep them clear of static activity and electro-gravitic accidents. The Kevlar suits had what could only be described as fishbowl headgear attachments, which made them all look like the robot from the 1950's movie 'The Day the Earth stood still'. These were to be worn only if EPACT required a venture outside the 'Object' or in the event of a life support failure. Despite hours of data studies and untold brainstorm sessions, there were still many unanswered questions. EPACT's only response to the non-returns' mystery, were the words 'insufficient capacity'. To this end its quantum computer circuits were quadrupled. EPACT's capacity now could encompass a wealth of human knowledge and creativity.

19th August 2020 launch day had finally arrived, and their specialist training barely contained the anxiety.

Dr Robert Smith, Marlin's top computer scientist and Control Room Manager, called on EPACT to initiate the primary field impulse generators and to take full control. The countdown sequence began with the monotonous voice of a computer generate. Magnetic fields created by the surrounding tesla coils hummed in unison, as the Obernauts laid in their bunks. Electric discharges danced in ribbons around the walls while static sparks and ozone smells ignited their senses. The monotonous unisex tone of EPACT's countdown reached zero. The launch was entering stage two, where the strong magnetic fields phased with gravity and blended these two major forces of nature into one. There was a sudden cessation of weight and all on board felt nauseous.

The nausea past in seconds and was replaced instantly with an intense feeling of euphoria and then abject silence. Arnold was looking across at Christian and was stunned, his face was glowing, and his hair was standing on end, like a twilight zone Bart Simpson with his finger in an outlet. Peabody fared no better, but as Arnold watched he started to float slightly off his bunk until his webbing harness automatically restrained him. The silence made Arnold think he was deaf, but the weightlessness they were all experiencing, and an enhanced feeling of wellbeing neutralised all fears. They were at peace.

Like a giant crushing spring the 'Object' was being charged. The rig platform was secured to the sea

floor's solid granite bedrock and additional tether-
ing via unbreakable titanium chains had been added.
At some point in the next few minutes, the 'Object'
reached a zenith point. It was a crucial crossover zone,
where on a subatomic level, loops of gravitons resonate with strings of electro-magnetic bosons. Then the
spring released.

EPACT acknowledged this transition with a short
verse; 'Object' migrating Space-time,' which seemed to
Arnold at the time, to underestimate the excitement
of their adventure. The weightlessness stopped for a
moment as the titanium coated bullet faded into no-
where land, subjectively through an open portal in the
floor of the rig and on into the gravity well of space-
time. Previous launches had shown that the 'Object'
blinked out as it touched the sea water and appeared
as a stationary shadow of its former self. The saline
water itself became part of the process at a subatomic
level, as did the silica within the igneous granite rock
base. There was no great splash nor a calamitous
crash into the ocean floor. At some point just before
time ceased to have meaning, Arnold thought that
they must have been surrounded in the calming salt
waters of Great Oyster Bay, as the sun set in its daily
ritual of glorious pink and orange hues. They all then
passed out.

Arnold awoke to the realisation that the three of
them, EPACT and the 'Object' now failed to exist in
terms of previous reality, so Arnold pinched himself
and it still hurt. A non-hour later EPACT had es-

tablished that the 'Objects' controls and life support systems were all functioning normal. They were now living in the time cone of a 13.5 by 7-metre silver bullet in no-where land, somewhere just outside space-time, but fortunately not in the cold waters of Great Oyster Bay. So far, their very existence exceeded their expectations. For just that moment when they all still existed. EPACT was responding in a most unsympathetic manner by repeating the phrase:

'Stay on the route provided.'

Arnolds two compatriots suddenly dissolved or faded out of view, just prior, he thought he heard Christian mumble something like:

'Oh yeah now I get it!'

He could not be sure. As these thoughts entered Arnold's mind, a bright white light with the texture of silk encompassed his body. The rear portal of the 'Object' then opened to reveal a gelatinous mass of bright purple goo, and Arnold heard EPACT complain:

'Control superseded by unknown algorithms, mission abort.'

Suddenly a noise in Arnold's mind went through a strange array of tweets, gurgles, and animated language sounds. This maelstrom of voice ended abruptly and after a moment of silence he heard a clear and concise message:

'Ωβ∑πμ-0010020015 - MUZE-directive Earth languages Anglo - Greetings Arnold!

Do not concern yourself about your fellow travelers, their essence has been absorbed by the MUZE. They are at peace and aware. Human beings are just a four-dimensional life form on the road of accelerated complexity. Your prepubescent science, that you use for destruction, is concerning to greater minds and may require some additional adjustment to our culling assessment plan'.

Arnold felt a degree of sadness at this statement, his thoughts were duplicating over and over, until he passed out again.

CHAPTER EIGHT

Subterfuge

B oris Podoloff was sitting in his office when the call came through from Moscow, the President demanded an urgent meeting, as further details had developed in relation to the investigation. Boris booked a flight and was in the Kremlin by 8am the next morning. A frigid wind was blowing off the Artic, and Boris was feeling the chill even under his Shuba of Mink. He waited in the outer office until he was called. The President's office was in the Kremlin Senate, a historic building built by order of Catherine the Great, it reeked of history and subterfuge. Boris was ordered to sit. The President was not happy:

'We have lost two great patriots, and I'm extremely annoyed. Comrade Dimitry went missing off this Refuge Island, just after sending through some valuable information, and Comrade Maxim was in contact just before returning to the submarine and he too has disappeared. We believe both men are dead. It seems there are things of great interest and extreme importance to our Federation on that Island development. Comrade Dimitri's last report is a recording of a conversation between this Marlin Jackson and his associate David Doyle. They are discussing an encounter with an alien intelligence via a metallic egg like device, that Jackson has had in his possession since he was a boy. It seems that your observation of that purple glowing light at university was correct Boris, I wish this information was acted on, by your father, from the outset.

Over the years this Australian Professor has acquired considerable details in relation to the mathematics of quantum gravity theory, and this is the reason their companies have made great strides. This device, that the aliens communicate with, is in Jackson's possession and we need to recover it; our great Federation cannot fall behind in these ultimate discoveries. We have our agent Sasha Fedovski in Canberra now, I do not care how he achieves it, but we must have this device. I am officially putting you in charge of this agent, come up with a plan and just make it happen Boris. Failure is not an option, for our Federation or for you.'

Boris left the office feeling sick in the stomach, the President had made a vailed threat, he was aware that Oligarchs and their wealth can disappear as quickly as the winter wind in this country.

Sasha Fedovski was sitting in his Canberra office, at the Russian Embassy, when the secure call came in from Moscow, it was Boris:

'Fedovski, this is Boris Podoloff in the Kremlin, I have a request, which comes straight from our President. I have been directed to manage you in a most important task. By this stage you should be well informed on this Marlin Jackson, and his Tasmanian enterprises. I require you to go there and gather as much knowledge as possible, this includes his family as well. He has an object we require. We believe it is metallic and the size of a duck egg. He always keeps it with him. I believe you should find a vulnerable path to this mission. Perhaps kidnapping a loved one for an exchange. Once you have accomplished this task, we will arrange a quick extraction of yourself, via diplomatic or direct means. Do not fail us, you know what to do if you are compromised, death would be a better option than returning home empty handed. Let me know when arrangements are made.

'Ya, comrade Boris, I understand and accept the mission. I have been informed of the sad loss of my fellow agents, I considered Dimitry to be a good friend, I will be successful on this mission, I owe them that. We have another agent here who can assist me. Roman Dubinsky, he has had experience in extracting information. May I use him in this venture?'

'I have no problem with how you go about this business, what we demand is success.'

'That is good. I have discovered much about this man Jackson. I believe he has a grandson, who will be the ideal exchange candidate. I believe the best way to achieve a safe Tasmanian exit, with the object, will be like the other agents arrival method. I will organise the necessary equipment to reach the submarine, and inform you of times, if you can organise the necessary pickup coordinates off the Freycinet Peninsula. Travelling back to Canberra, even with our diplomatic clearances could be problematic with the current Covid-19 restrictions. One man may be alright, but two could lead to questions'

'Ya, Sasha I concur, I will make the arrangements, good luck comrade.'

CHAPTER NINE

Us and the Universe balloon

'I am Arnold Bask; I report now under a veil of trepidation. I have lost something within my unconscious state. I know, it or what, was there, and I know in some way I was helping it find answers, but what was the result? I can still hear the voice':

'MUZE-directive Earth languages Anglo - Greetings Arnold!'

Arnold woke up in a hospital bed in Hobart. He was conscious, but his subconscious self was also, and he knew he was not in full control. Orders of a mission were overlaying his human will, and his individuality was being compromised. He mumbled an abstract thought:

'A culling assessment plan', that made him nauseous again, as he fell into a soft purple glutinous bed.

'What a strange world': thought Arnold-MUZE, the other self, as he drifted through a strange dream:

'In the beginning, there was zilch, nada, nothing, basically no space.'

Real Arnold now sensed his other self, as a God or an Allah or even Jehovah. So, in his dream state on that soft purple bed, he had a vision:

'A special mind gift was given to him; it was a strange object called a Universe Balloon. It was a wonder of creation. He put the Universe Balloon to his lips and began to blow hard'.

This inflating effort gave Arnold-MUZE, three things: the upper hand of control in the brain department of real Arnold, a need to meet Marlin, prior to the culling assessment plan on humanity, and lastly after a healthy consultation period an overwhelming need for a substance called beer.

The staff on Refuge Island were all in shock over the disappearance of Nick Peabody, and Christian Taylor. The critical issue now was Arnold and his health. A formal memorial for the missing two Obernauts would be held later. The Object was shut down and moth balled until a full study of events could take place.

Marlin was at the bed side of Arnold-MUZE, as he awoke:

'Good, you're awake, how do you feel Arnold?'

Marlin watched Arnold's expressions, his facial features flickered between frowns and smiles. His eyes were blinking rapidly, and they were changing colour from bright blue to a soft purple. His vital signs were steady. Arnold took a few seconds to adjust, and responded:

'You can still call me Arnold-MUZE if you like, names have no real concept in our realm. You must be Marlin Jackson, greetings, it is good to meet you. We are pleased you received all our messages. We were always aware that a few of your species had the possibility of some understanding.'

Marlin stood there in stunned silence. He was never sure of what the outcomes would be of all his scientific developments. His whole life was determined by the incident in 1952, when the 'Object' first appeared. From time to time over the years, throughout his studies the 'Object' would glow and reveal formulars and mathematical concepts that helped him obtain his great knowledge and wealth, but the recall of Arnolds first wakening words:

'A culling assessment plan.'

Now created anxiety in the mind of Marlin Job Jackson, had he invited death to dinner?

Arnold's life as an Obernaut was on hold, the new Arnold-MUZE needed a plan and some earthly adjustment. This all took a while. Marlin and a team of specialists kept Arnold-MUZE in isolation, while planning various interviews. They had long philosophical conversations on humanity, its history, both the good and the bad, the concepts of war and peace, and the strangeness of love and hate. Marlin provided Arnold-MUZE many books and videos of life on Earth.

Arnold-MUZE, commented that some of the earlier human advances in physics and chemistry had pre-cipitated their interest in our species. He took it all in and came to realise that his mission would involve an understanding of all of humanity. Marlin, although nervous of outcomes, decided to assist Arnold-MUZE in this quest. Although it was not mentioned by Mar-lin or his team, this new Arnold stressed that they were aware of the human expansions, into the world of sub-atomic interactions, and that the human dis-covery of gravitational waves, was a major step.

'You have much to learn and we have much to talk of,' said Arnold-MUZE.

Arnold-MUZE was adamant, with Marlin, that the process should be totally random. There was no point in meeting with a select group of intellectuals and academics. What had to happen was, for us to develop a general view of the attitude of the world public. To this end Marlin suggested that a tour throughout the Country would be an effective way to achieve this outcome. Having landed in Tasmania, a tour of the Australian mainland could be easily sponsored. This Nation was now a melting pot of multicultural Earth, there would be no better place on the planet to con-duct such a random tour. Arnold-MUZE could get an understanding of the future of humanity, and hopefully come to a happy conclusion about our worth in the greater scheme.

Despite reservations in Marlin's mind, and his personal view of narrow-minded business and political short-term interest, there was the chance that Arnold-MUZE might witness more of the good, and less of the bad. The question of direction in the advent of more human scientific discoveries, could only come if this visitor witnessed a greater percentage of goodwill in the populace. Any malcontent in the human psyche, that could lead to a destructive desire for a future virulent apocalyptic conquest of the Galaxy, would not discourage the cull's continuance.

Arnold-MUZE was now the voice, the judge, and the jury of his symbiotic species. Marlin was not aware of this, he thought alien Arnold would have to report his findings and not be the one to initiate the cull. Marlin assumed their only way out of a cull, was by showing that humans in general were an empathetic species of freewill and advanced social consciousness. He was not overconfident in the task ahead, but believed that the human inhabitants of Earth, were just as important in the matrix of life as Arnold-MUZE very own existence. He hoped they would see this because an opposite outcome was unthinkable. To say that this new Arnold was just a part of a whole, a fifth dimensional consciousness in a MUZE society, would be an oversimplification, and could not be put into words that Marlin would completely understand. Arnold-

MUZE was objective, and from the back of his joint mind, he looked into Marlin's eyes and said:

'The glass is still half full, at this stage mate, and I still have this overwhelming need for that beer!'

Marlin felt that was a promising idea. To work out a random way of contact was their next task, so a walk around Hobart and a chat at a Pub might be an effective way to start.

CHAPTER TEN

Time for a beer

Rachelle Castle's report of the incident at Wineglass Bay was kept under wraps by the department. The Minister was also made aware, but because of the pandemic and other world tensions with the USA and China, the Refuge Island issue went cold from government.

Nothing ever went cold at D.O.N.T, they were still on the case. There was now concern that Dr Marlin Jackson's project was far more than what they were told, so monitoring the site would be stepped up. The magnetic disturbances had ceased, and satellite reconnaissance had shown no activity on Refuge Island. There were reports of an exodus of staff from the Freycinet Lodge and applications for transfers offshore. There were also rumours of missing persons, that related to some of the staff from the Island. A recent death certificate was lodged for a Jim Hunter, who was said to have died from natural causes. This was signed off by a doctor employed by Jackson's company. The suspicions around this project were rising daily and two days ago and ambulance moved persons unknown to a Private Hospital facility in Hobart also owned by Jackson's Company. Rachelle Castles was deployed to Hobart to conduct further investigations.

The Hobart Hope and Anchor Tavern claims to be the oldest established hotel in Australia, with the first rum drunk in 1807. This could be a true statement. Marlin's fisherman ancestry had its birth in this town. They were whalers and sealers, until they found God, and Kangaroo Island. Arnold looked around the tavern museum. Although his body had frequented this place often over the years, the new Arnold and his MUZE were seeing it anew. The ancient sea faring artifacts and stories of conquest, survival, and whale slaughter were totally alien concepts, but the books and videos he had read and seen in the hospital about life on Earth, had given some perception and clarity.

Just as Rachelle Castles settled into her motel accommodation at the Mercure in Hobart, a message and photo appeared on her phone. It came via Intel services to D.O.N.T headquarters, indicating that:

'Marlin Jackson, picture attached, was tracked and located via his mobile phone to the Hobart Hope and Anchor Tavern'.

It was just what Rachelle needed, a reason to relax a little with a wine after the flight and conduct some surveillance.

Arnold had his back to the door and Rachelle missed seeing him as she walked in. Marlin bought the first round, a good-looking lady caught his eye, but his focus was on questioning Arnold. He returned with two mid-strength beers. The part of Arnold-MUZE that longed for an ale was set well back in the mind of the real Arnold, still he did enjoy the taste of this beer. Marlin explained the history of alcohol on the planet, as best he could, and stressed its inebriating danger. He told Arnold that substantial amounts of alcohol took away inhibitions, and that sometimes made human interaction difficult. Some people became addicts to alcohol, which could cause the onset of family violence and even death. There were even worse drugs that humans profited from at the expense of society. Arnold listened intently, Marlin went on to explain that humans are complicated primates, many mean well and have a great deal of empathy for all creatures on Earth. All people are born good, with survival instincts that can lead to greed, selfishness and sometimes evil. We also can educate and find solutions to problems, given time, good will always prevails. Marlin looked at Arnold-MUZE and smiled:

'For the moment let us just get to know each other'.

The small amount of alcohol that Arnold-MUZE and

Marlin had consumed, began to wash away some inhibitions. Their bonding had evolved over the past
few weeks and trust was building. The collective audience within Arnold felt it too. Arnold-MUZE felt the
need to understand this man, that his species had provided with such advanced technology.

Marlin was in deep concentration listening to Arnold-MUZE's every word. Rachelle glanced in their
direction and was shocked for a moment, she just
realised that it was Arnold from the café talking to
Marlin. From her previous encounter with Arnold,
she thought he was just an electrician on the island.
She knew he had seen her, and her cover was now
blown, but strangely although they only had brief eye
contact, it did not register with him who she was. Rachelle took her wine and sat in an alcove out of site
of the two men, but close enough to pick up the occasional word.

Both were unaware that the lady at the bar had
moved and was picking up snippets of their conversation, Marlin then asked a fundamental question:

'Marlin you have a profound knowledge in the fields
of electro-gravitics, electro-kinetics and particle physics. You succeeded, with our limited help, to develop
Entangled Particle Morse and to send travellers beyond the threshold of space-time, but what do you
think your existence means?'

'That question, Arnold, is at the centre of most of the research that humans carry out. From our time as primitive hunter gatherers we have stared at the heavens and pondered that question. It led to our beliefs in supreme beings, the creation of faith base religions, tools, art, culture and eventually the scientific process. The values of scientific knowledge far outweigh our own short lives, so we passed on our research with learning establishments and the written word. We still can only speculate on a reason for existence. I have used the analogy that intelligence is a cactus flower in the desert of space-time, that flourishes and withers away as nature intended.

If there was an internal puppeteer of the Great-Out-Doors, a G.O.D that predetermines everything that has or will happen, it would have to occupy the centre of every single sub-atomic particle and create material substance right through to biological thought. Some people think this could be a Universe by design. Up until now I believe it is a natural continuing process that occurred via a negative and positive energy imbalance.

If the creation of a biological life form, who can strive to understand their existence through thought and tools is a natural process, then its place in our present physical and material time cone evolves, probably until another catastrophic extinction event. We could be just a projection of frozen energy caught in the gravity well of space-time, billions of years from the seeds of our creation and never quite within reach of our purpose. Science research and an Occam's Razor approach to obvious causal outcomes have found potential intelligent results. They included: deep ocean thermal vents, a primordial swamp of amino acids, and a vigorous radioactive and electrostatic atmosphere. This activity may have brought about a compound that led to RNA, then to a basic DNA ladder of ongoing exponential instructions from extremophiles to primates.

The building blocks may also have been delivered by hydro-carbon comets in the early Solar System at its foundation four billion years ago. All of this is possible in an infinite universe with infinite cause and effect, even if probability factors are extremely high. In our present time cone, most scientists believe we came from a subatomic singularity, called the Big Bang, beyond which there could be an ongoing process without a time factor. That Arnold, and your gift of an 'Object', is why finding reason and logic in existence became my life's work.

In my early years at University, I had philosophical thoughts on the subject. I remember looking at a spinning ceiling fan and how the strobe effect of matching frequency made the fan stop. I thought of unobserved electrons moving from solids to waves, subject to observation. Then remembering my basic physics and the Law of Resonance, where the rate of the vibration projected, will harmonize with, and attract back energies with the same resonance. I thought that this somehow related to the two-slot experiment, where wave function of subatomic particles changed subject to observation.

We delved into super symmetry, string theory, vibrating branes of resonance that built the sub-atomic world, and then finally M-theory, that showed in concept a multiverse of eleven dimensions. Then our CERN collider found a Higgs Bosun, a sub-atomic building block that collated matter. All this proton bombardment and the madness of speculation and math had me thinking about reality, not a sky-father inspired view of retro causality, observed from random time points, but something a little bit simpler, 'matter projection'.

I once learnt that all matter is energy in stasis and at the speed of light all matter becomes energy. Albert Einstein gave us $E = MC^2$ without an inclusive explanation of gravity, other than time dilation. Then the Quantum world gave up its secret of spooky action-at-a-distance, that exists and can be used in Quantum computing. Now you have come along from some dimension that has no real meaning in our cosmos view of existence. Are you our creators Arnold, and does your species live in a time cone of its own?'

The MUZE collective via Arnold pondered Marlin's comments and his question, and an answer surfaced:

'I will answer the first part of your question Marlin, the second part will be answered in due course, but first may I have another glass of this delightful ale?'

Marlin laughed to himself; the original Arnold would have just said your shout mate!

The beer came and Arnold-MUZE continued:

'Do we live in a time cone of its own, you asked? 'I will answer that in a way that you may find overly simplistic, but logical to your human thought processes. Our time is non-linear, and as infinite as the size of your universe, it is at a right angle to your perception abilities. You alone know this because your 'Object' stepped out of the time you exist in. Real Arnold perceived us as a purple biological glutinous mass, and your EPACT computer equated that its control had been superseded by unknown algorithms. We see all, as you have already stated, a view of retro causality observed from random time points. We are one with biology and algorithms, and we too evolved to our present state from a previous four-dimensional existence. We make errors in judgement, we were one hundred years out for your arrival, but we correct and collude as one. Let us explain to you who we are. You know us as the MUZE, we exist outside your reality, and we know we have purpose.

There are many unknowns about our creation. It occurred at the junction of two universes collid-

ing. It was initiated as an experiment by an advanced artificial intelligence society that survived on
matter. Everything we can see is made of this ba-
ryonic matter, and it only accounts for five percent
of the Universe. The rest is dark matter, probably
sterile neutrinos, and the gravity defying dark energy.
Finding the words to explain this in human terms is
difficult. We are based on algorithmic energy and a
biological plasma outside your spacetime, in a realm
that you would call the fifth dimension. That dimension is wrapped up in a cone of unexplainable anti-
dark-matter held in place by anti-dark-energy. We believe this is what sustains our group mind. We see all
the life energy in your universe. There are a billion
stars in your galaxy and there are a billion galaxies in
your universe, and life abounds. In that vast cosmos
there is only one place where human beings evolved,
and that is Earth. We believe that you may have instigated that artificial intelligence society that led to
our creation, but there are other types of beings in
your universe who are capable as well. We monitor
all, our very existence depends on undisturbed time-
cones and temporal balance.

We can continue this discussion when we return
from a fact-finding tour. We wish to fine positive purpose, and an overview of your cultural consciousness
before conclusion of our first impressions.'

Marlin now felt like he had lost something in trans-
lation, their statement:

'Conclusion of our first impressions.'

Made him feel that perhaps he had been used, and even a traitor to humankind.

'I have one further question Arnold, our three missing Obernauts, where are they? Are they dead?'

'No Marlin that's not how our symbiosis works, in your concept of us, they have been absorbed into the whole of us, they are now the MUZE. So, they are part of the group who make the decisions, and as such will offer input, that could be to your advantage.

They finished off the beers and made their way back to Marlin's office. All Arnolds travel passes, and arrangements had been made. He was given flexibility in the destinations, but Victoria was still in a full Covid-19 lockdown, so NSW would be his first port of call. His flight to Sydney was a garbled affair, conversations were limited because of face masks and fear.

Rachelle left shortly after the men. She had only a limited knowledge of physics but was astounded at some of the language she had heard; like entangled particle morse and sending travellers beyond the threshold of space-time. The words, 'Does your species live in a time cone of its own?' and 'they have been absorbed into the whole of us, they are now the muse.'

were the real standout to her. It was now obvious to Rachelle that there was more to this mining operation than rare earth minerals and this fellow Arnold had to be monitored as well.

CHAPTER ELEVEN

D.O.N.T follow me

Rachelle left the Hobart Hope and Anchor Tavern and went back to her motel. She then rang Ian Evans on a secure line.

D.O.N.T Director Ian Evans at H.Q in Canberra was feeling anxious. It was an extremely hot October day. Ian was not into suits unless he had meetings with ministers. Today he was dressed for the heat, a Panama hat, island shirt, Bermuda shorts and Aviator glasses. The handmade Franciscan Italian sandals finished off the cool look. He was more like Danny De-Vito in a Copacabana beach shack, than a top spy boss. Ian was sitting at his favourite Cafe on the banks of Lake Burley Griffin, sipping a lime and soda when the phone rang.

'Ian? It's Rachelle, we have a problem, the project on

Refuge Island is not a mining operation, it's some sort of device to bring aliens to our planet'.

'Come on Rachelle don't play games like that you'll end up in the psych ward'.

'No, I'm serious, and I have heard conversations that no one would believe. I need to get closer to this Arnold Bask. He is not just the electrician he said he was, when I met him at Coles Bay, he is some sort of traveller. I only picked up snippets of his conversation with Marlin Jackson. There was a lot of talk about quantum physics and devices that Marlin had developed. Then the shock came, I heard Marlin ask Arnold if his species live in a time cone of its own. There was also a mention that others that had been absorbed into something called the muse. This is not the Arnold I met, and another thing, he eye-balled me, without recognition.'

'This sounds like some sort of way-out conspiracy theory Rachelle, they may be having you on, you did say that Mr Bask spotted you. Either way, you're on site, so I suggest you tail him and gather more information. There must be something on that island that they are trying to cover up, and misinformation is always a tool in that department. I will initiate a full investigation on Marlin Jackson from my end. Be safe and keep me posted. By the way we failed to find any sign of your missing Russian, and Pine Gap reports the sub is no longer in the area.'

Through D.O.N.T sources in Border Force, Rachelle
managed to get all of Arnold's flight plans. His first
stop was Sydney. Going to Melbourne first was out
of the question, a Covid-19 lockdown was in force
to stop the Pandemic spreading throughout the community. This would have limited Arnold's ability to
communicate with people. Rachelle followed Arnold
in a cab from the airport to a motel in Phillip Street
Parramatta. She now knew his base of operation, so
booked herself into another motel around the corner.
It would not be a problem if Rachelle lost him, because
of Covid-19 restrictions, tracking was easy. Arnold
played by the rules of law. He nominated on all his
travel documents, the locations that he may be staying at, where possible. Although he left it open to
changes when required. Wherever he went he used
the QR systems and that was another means of tracking him.

Arnold-MUZE, noticed the motel had a bar as he
entered. He dropped off his gear to his room and went
back for a beer. The bar service person was a pretty
lady named Brenda. She was a backpacker from Ire-
land, who was now trapped in Australia because of the
pandemic. He was the only person in the room and
talked with Brenda at length. She was from Belfast,
and she spoke of all the previous troubles in her glorious land. A beautiful land she described as:

'Forty shades of green, but the religious rivalry had

set like concrete. The hate, the revenge and all the sad unnecessary killings, had seen a vast number leave for a better life in a less volatile place. Australia was the answer to their problems.'

It was a sad tale, but she recalled things were changing and the violence had ebbed of late, and hope was on the horizon. Arnold-MUZE was taken in by her forthright and bright manner. He knew the story of the previous potato famine and forced convict departures, after reading up on Australian history. This new information gave him insight to human folly, sadness, and desire for a better life. He finished up the beer, thanked Brenda for her story and went for a walk-up Parramatta's main street.

Rachelle checked in and freshened up. She then went for a walk back towards Arnolds Motel and sat in a café on the opposite side of the street. It was a beautiful 19th century building fully restored with French windows and a garden. As she finished her coffee Arnold walked out of his motel and headed towards the centre of the city, she followed him.

This Church Street as it was called, was a construction zone. High-rise development, cranes and men in Hi-Viz and helmets were everywhere. Arnold-MUZE stopped and chatted to people as he walked. Some were too busy, some spoke with the excitement of having a job in the Covid-19 shutdown, and others were wary as to what he was selling or pushing. A new light rail system was being constructed down Church Street, and it was like a giant snake slowly devouring the businesses as it progressed. Shops were shut and For-Lease signs festooned the footpath. Things changed drastically as he approached Town Hall and a stunning early settlement church. In front was the rail interchange and the huge shopping complex.

Arnold-MUZE recalled Marlin's words:

'You won't just discover Australia in Parramatta you will find the world. Western Sydney is the multicultural heartland of the Nation, it is a breadbasket of worldly identities and an ideal place for you to get a perspective of human inhabitants.'

Saint John's Church in Parramatta is the oldest church in Australia, sitting in a wonderful park setting, surrounded by a growing city of high-rise buildings and exponential development. A growth not held back by the pandemic; it was now a city of construction. It was a perfect place for an investigation of people. They were all Australians, but from all over the world. There were Indian and European men sitting in groups chatting at tables in front of cooling water sprouts, with children playing in the mist. There were Asian women doing their daily tai-chi exercises, there were Middle Eastern families feeding pigeons in front of the church. There were women and men in skirts and suits making their way to their office works. There were others in coveralls heading for construction sites.

As Arnold walked, he passed street vendors and buskers. Amongst all these people, moved families, vagrants, sightseers, criminals, and Christian pamphlet pushers. It was an Australian mosaic of cosmopolitan living, and for a man on a mission it was the perfect situation. Arnold watched people and listened to their conversations. Occasionally he would ask directions and start-up a chat. Rachelle always followed at a safe distance, listening, and watching his every move.

Arnold, and his internally captive audience, started to see that the humans, in general, were both happy and contented. Their lot in life seemed to be somewhat philosophical, along the lines of whatever happens, happened for a reason. Despite some issues of finance, and unrequited love, the happy memories of childhood shone through. They had the occasional fights with their partners, friends, and neighbours, but in general most people seem to be happy. There was the other side of the divide as well. People affected by domestic violence or the criminal order. Some dealt in drugs that sent others on paths of destruction. There were also people who sponsored overseas unfortunates, to work in sweatshops or to be sold off as sex slaves.

Aside from all the negatives, there was this overall desire for happiness, as it was the greatest wish.

There was a saying that summed it up, Arnold had read it on a Leunig calendar:

'A life well lived in was a life well died in.'

In many, this happiness was supported by the countless religions, cults, and beliefs. Arnold found that this multicultural heartland had a vast number of supreme deity believers. He was amazed to find out that there were one-hundred and fifty Government recognised religions in Australia. Although thirty percent of the population had no religion, and this number was growing. Some people were agnostic, and many were atheists. The mainstream religions held the biggest number of parishioners. Amongst these there were cults that were only there to serve as wealth generators for their leaders. Much of this information was already known by the MUZE, but it still came across as strange. Humans, through science, had achieved so much knowledge of the world and their place in it, yet the inconsistencies and hypocrisy of the bulk of humanity was astounding.

Two traits shone through in these discussions: empathy and the concepts of love. The Greek civilisation had named seven kinds of love, Philia, Eros, Storge and Agape, being the Philosopher Plato's main four. The MUZE appreciated Storge, the universal empathy bond. The other three; Philia, brotherly love, Eros romantic and sexual love, and Agape unconditional love, had no concept in their asexual five-dimensional consciousness.

Arnold spent the entire day chatting and talking to diverse groups of people. Rachelle thought it was strange the way some people would open-up to him and tell their whole life stories. Some would just walk away thinking he was a salesman or a religious pest. Others were indifferent and maybe had just a few words. The ones who lingered, talked at length about where they came from and what their values were, and where they wanted to be in the future. All up it was a good indication of life in a free country. There was enormous potential here, for the people who would work hard to feel a sense of achievement.

It was getting on in the afternoon, so Arnold decided it was time for another beer. He found his way to a hotel called the Woolpack Inn. This Inn had one of the oldest licences in Australia, dating back to 1796. Arnold could sense its atmosphere and he noted the crowd were different here. They were mainly the Anglo/Celtic Australians, the conversations here were all sports related. Arnold-MUZE sat there in the bar and ordered a schooner of a mid-strength ale. Both enjoyed this drink, but it was the taste buds of the real Arnold, not the MUZE. Rachelle saw this as an opportunity, so she made her way to a stool near Arnold at the bar. She sat there for a while hoping he would remember her. He smiled but there was no recognition. This seemed odd because they did have quite an attraction when they first met. Arnold had gained a little knowledge on how to manage situations. He did not let on that he had seen her watching him over the last few days. He said hello and started with the all-time favourite ice breaker:

'Hi, I'm Arnold, great weather isn't it.'

The two touched elbows, the current Covid-19 greeting in NSW:

'Nice to meet you Arnold, I'm Rachelle, this time of the year is always the best in Parramatta, just before the heat starts. Are you a local?' She enquired.
'No, just passing through, I'm interested in people's opinion to the current Covid-19 crisis, for a research group I work for. What about you?'

Rachelle changed her story a little:

'I'm a librarian from Hobart, I'm stranded here in Parramatta now, because of the pandemic travel bans.'

'This story change did not even register with him.' She thought. 'What's happened to him, maybe he is an alien, I swear his eyes just went from bright blue to a purple glint.'

They chatted for a while about Arnold's research. He told her that he was surveying the population mix in western Sydney and afterwards he would travel around the countryside to gain the perspective of others:

'Seeing people and talking about where they had come from, what their ambitions were and how they are managing the pandemic was a fun job. They all chat for a while about the weather and then some people just can't stop talking, it's like some sort of release, and extremely interesting to us.'

Rachelle smiled:
'You just said 'interesting to us', you must be very dedicated to your company?'

Yes, very dedicated.' Smiled Arnold, and continued:
'What are you doing for dinner tonight?'
'I am hungry, what do you have in mind? My motel, the Park Royal, is two blocks from here, it has a high-quality restaurant in the foyer. We could go there. It would be great to chat a little longer.

Well, is it a date Rachelle?' said Arnold finishing his beer.

'Ok by me, I'll see you at 7pm in the foyer.'

All the time that Arnold was watching her, he felt a strange kind of feeling come over him. This not only affected Arnold it affected the MUZE as well, but there was also a definite physical attraction here, that neither he nor the collective could understand. The MUZE had the ability to follow an individual's timeline.   They were reluctant to use this method, as it could create unwarranted time distortions.   Due to the investigation into human potential, they used it with Marlin, Arnold, and some previous attempts. Since meeting with Rachelle, the MUZE had a taste of something that they had never experienced before. It came via Arnolds thought processes and physiological changes in his body. Apart from strange reactions, they now were aware that Rachelle was not who she said she was. She was on a mission from her government.

Marlin Jackson was caught unaware of the surprise visit. It is not every day that the Premier of the State comes calling.   Dr Robert Smith was still on site at Refuge Island and David Doyle was in Hobart. The facility and EPACT programmes were still active, but with a reduced staff. They only had an hour to talk about the pending visit and their response, it was obvious that there had been a leak:

'The cat is out of the bag' said Marlin, 'how do we spin this one?'

Smith pondered for a minute: 'I think we should sell the 'Object' as a new propulsion system. This new anti-gravity, magnetic tech has enormous potential.'

'Yes,' replied Marlin, 'we may be able to use gravity

reversal for 'Object' thrust, to place satellites in orbit. We could say that the reason for the cover up was due to our commercial interests, and that certain states may see it has a military potential. This project will offer great prosperity and environmental stability to Tasmania and mainland Australia. I believe our Green Premier will accept our reasoning, don't you?'

Smith stared at Marlin with a sullen expression:

'What about the alien encounter? What if they know about Arnold?

'We will play that by ear. We can say that all our tethered tests have been conducted with extreme risk protocols and procedures. We needed the primate and follow-up human occupants to ascertain that the electro-gravitic effects are not detrimental to human health.

The Premier arrived and he was accompanied by the Director of the Department of National Threats, Ian Evans, this occasion warranted a suit. It was obvious now to Marlin that there had been a leak, and information about the true nature of his programme had been exposed. Marlin decided, it would be smart if prior to the meeting, he gave a tour of the project. It was the best way to sell the story they prepared. Ian Evans was up front while looking at the 'Object' and the hi-tech equipment that surrounded it. He alluded to the fact that his group had analysts look at pictures of the site, and they concluded it was not a drilling project.

Both men were impressed with what they saw, especially the Control Room.

The Premier sat opposite Marlin in the briefing room, with the two other men adjacent. He laid out the planned explanation of the projects true purpose and the real potential of the new propulsion system. Both visitors seemed to understand. The Premier was not happy about the need to not brief him from the start, but when Smith talked about the project's great prosperity potential and environmental stability, the Premier seemed hooked, but he did comment on the project apparent slowing progress:

'You seem to be running on a skeleton staff Professor, is the project close to completion?'

'No Premier, we are going through a data assessment phase, this is a prototype development. Its looking good now, and we may be in a position for a test launch, if we ever get over this Covid-19 menace.'

Evans was more circumspect. His first comment was about foreign interference, he told the men about CIA reports, the Russian submarine interest, and the possible death of an agent off Refuge Island. Marlin was shocked by this revelation, he responded:

'Our security manager James Brennan was given details by one of our staff about two foreign nationals. They were looking suspicious on the Hazzard Trail. No one has followed up with us re that encounter, as yet'.

'That's correct Professor, we too are not always free with correct information on our enquiries. We had an agent investigate and she met with one of your electricians an Arnold Bask. We are also aware that you met with him in Hobart, and you were heard having a very strange conversation. Can you explain an alien reference, and something about people being absorbed by the muse?'

'I'm not sure about the alien reference, but if that was the same agent in Hobart who Arnold met at Coles Bay, he possibly recognised her. He is a character with the ladies and knowing Arnold he probably mentioned a few left field things in our private discussion to amuse himself. Our staff are trained not to divulge information on the project and that's why he said he was an electrician. He actually is an Electrical Engineer and a team leader in our in-craft assessment group.'

'Would it be possible to talk with Arnold now Professor?'
'No sorry, Arnold is on leave now in New South Wales on a personal special interest project.'

Evans was assessing the theory that there may be two Arnolds, he was aware of Rachelle's thoughts, that the Arnold she was trailing was a different man and he respected his agent's ability

The meeting ended with Covid-19 knuckle touches all round. The Premier seemed placated, but Evans was doubtful, something was still not right, but he was happy to leave Rachelle on the case. When the visitors left, Marlin and Smith looked at each other and smiled:

'Great work Professor, you played that well.'

CHAPTER TWELVE

Strange love

The date at the Park Royal would be a strange encounter. Two people concealing identities, over dinner and a friendly chat, was not going to be easy. Rachelle walked into the dining room looking stunning. She was wearing a fetching low cut saffron coloured dress with frangipani flowers on the hem. Her yellow stilettos gave her the height of an Amazonian Princess. There was no need and no room for a weapon. She was thinking about the Arnold she met at the Café at Coles Bay and the attraction she had for him. Her mind was analysing the lead up events:

'This was not that same man. Has he been brain washed? or is he playing games'

Arnold arrived dressed in denim jeans and a sports shirt, his manly frame was a good match with this woman's delicate features. At his first glance of Rachelle, Arnold's heart skipped a beat: 'She is gorgeous, and I am underdressed'.

These were strange thoughts for Arnold and the MUZE, they were coming from the back of his mind. When it came to physiological feelings, they seemed to be manifested in the sub consciousness of real Arnold. The enjoyment was something they all shared.

Arnold and Rachelle exchanged greetings, had some small talk about the accommodation, and ordered their meals. They agreed on a ten-year old shiraz and that helped settle their anxieties. They both stuck to their stories. Rachelle was very talkative, she felt relaxed around this man. She told Arnold of her childhood growing up in Parramatta. She was an avid Eels rugby league fan. With her girlfriends from Parramatta High School, they spent most of their summer holidays at the Parramatta memorial pool. They would dive from the top tower, play water polo, or just lounge about on the grass taking in the summer sun.

Arnold sat there silently taking in every word, watching her lips move and her eyes sparkle. She spoke of many old memories; flirting with boys, yo-yos, hula-hoops, strawberry milkshakes, and fish and chips wrapped in newspaper. Then on a serious note, her tone turned a bit angry, she recalled the fight they had to stop the government tearing down their War Memorial pool to build a new stadium. Even though her beloved Eels would play there, the old stadium did the job required. It was just the starting point, she said:

'As you have seen Arnold, Parramatta is now a construction zone and I fear it will be years before all the dust settles. Anyhow, enough about me where did you grow up Arnold?'

For a moment, the MUZE froze, they had been so besotted by her expressions. There was a subconscious battle brewing in the joint mind. At times, the real Arnold would come back with the answers:

'Summer Hill in Sydney, it was a wonderful place to live. It was a tough area, but I had great mates. We weren't bad kids, but we did get up to some mischief. We would hoon around on our bikes or skateboards, between the memorial park and the town centre fountain. On some nights we would sneak out and spray paint our graffiti tags on railway billboards. Other times we would catch a train to Central and make our way down to the Harbour with our fishing gear. In summer we all caught the train to Cronulla and surfed all day. We did have fights, there were lots of diverse cultures in the area. There was also a bit of racism back then, and that triggered a few punch ups. It was the reason I learnt to defend myself at the local Police Boys Club. I was lucky, my mum was a stickler for a full education. She was into Blues music and one of her favourite artists was B King. He once quoted; 'The beautiful thing about learning is that no one can take it away from you.' She must have told me that a thousand times. So, I ended up with a decent education and an electrical career.'

It was Rachelle's turn to listen and wonder, this man was all she desired, but there was something about his eyes and the way his thoughts flickered. He had bright blue eyes and that was a great attraction, but at times when he frowned, they had what she thought was a purple glint, it was a strange thing. She put it down to the restaurant lighting or perhaps the Shiraz going to her head a little, but it did not matter she was feeling great attraction to this man and decided to go all the way.

The second bottle of wine, after a fine meal, was all it took. Their inhibitions dropped and sensual feelings took over:

'Would it be to forward of me to invite you back to my room for a coffee Arnold?'

The MUZE were just witnesses now, real Arnold was having a pheromone rush. He reached over and held her hand, their first touch was electric:

'I believe I could follow you anywhere.' He smiled and his blue eyes were back.

The bill was paid, and he followed this beautiful woman to her room. The night was just beginning.

Following the coffee, Rachelle excused herself to slip into something more comfortable. Arnold was sitting on the edge of the bed, half knowing what to expect, and thinking he should be bold and prepare. He was like a boy sitting in a school room, swooning over the prettiest girl in class. He had stripped down to his bright blue Calvin Klein undies, with his black socks still on. His manhood was erect, which was a shock to the MUZE within. The pheromone uptake negated bodily and mind control, the feeling to the group-mind was ecstasy in waiting. Rachelle exited her bathroom stark naked under a chiffon nighty, with a smile that would melt butter. Arnold looked at her with lust, she was gorgeous and shimmered all over with a coating of some exotic lotion. Her smell and sexuality so inviting that Arnold-MUZE experienced a strange nervous shivering in his body. The sex began in trepidation, minutes later she yelled with a tidal wave of passion.

They had three sessions that night, the last an hour of love, lust, and pleasure. Arnold and the MUZE mind were on a high, they had discovered their intimate Eros love and to their surprise, the instant uncondi-tional Agape love of soul mates. They laid for an hour smothered by the captivating smells of sex and sweet lotions. Rachelle laughed a lot, and then her demean-our fluctuated between looks of wanting and smiles of delight. Arnold was on a curve of awe, and the MUZE were re-evaluating their thoughts of humans. Perhaps, after hearing the lives of the humans Arnold was interviewing, they were starting to understand and find some brotherly love as well.

Rachelle and Arnold were both fit people and early risers. They awoke in good moods, and although not discussing the previous night's torrid love making, they both needed a morning walk. Rachelle was born in Northmead and knew the area well. She suggested a bush walk around Lake Parramatta. Arnold quickly agreed. The MUZE within shared the enthusiasm, they now hungered for these strange earthly experiences. They shared a light breakfast at the motel and headed off. Rain from the previous day had dampened the eucalypt forest. As they approached a dam wall, the smell of the fresh-water lake, damp leaf litter and summer burnt wood, heightened their senses. Arnold was stunned that such a forest and lake could be in the heart of a metropolis. Rachelle informed him that the creek was dammed in 1856 to provide a fresh supply of water for Parramatta. As they walked on, the early morning sun filtered through the ghost gums and iron barks. The lake was alive with shags and wild ducks. Arnold stopped suddenly as a large goanna ran from a towering termite mound. The scratch marks at its base indicated that it was the goannas breakfast bowl.

Rachelle was in a chatty mood and told Arnold about the Aboriginal history of the area. The MUZE's knowledge of human colonisation was now in full focus. The Colonists dam water had covered the once lived-in shelter caves. The Aboriginal timeline, showing hand stencils, stone flaking tools, and food middens, were all now hidden from view at this location. This contrast of human habitation, from a fifty -thousand- year history to a vast new City down-stream, was reason enough for some in the MUZE collective to move on with their main mission.

After the walk Arnold went about his business of interviews in the street and Rachel went back to her motel room. They both arranged to meet again for dinner that evening. Rachel was not keen to contact Ian Evans, because at this stage of her investigation she was having confusing thoughts. Deep down she felt she had to be honest with Arnold. Her feelings for him had grown considerably, but she had to ask the questions that had been bothering her.

Arnold and his MUZE mind collective were still ana- lysing the previous night's activities. Just after lunch Arnold went for a drink at another local pub. He asked a straight-forward friendly question to one pa- tron walking past:

'How-ya-goin-mate, what's through there? Arnold was pointing at a black curtain covering a door.'

For some reason, the bloke took instant offence at the inquiry:

'Private party ya-nosy-prick keep out.' Was the re- sponse.

The nasty rebuke did not faze Arnold, the guy was probably a tad drunk, he just smiled and sipped his beer. They eyeballed each other as the guy walked through the curtain. What Arnold was not aware of was that a local biker's chapter, had booked out the Poker machine room, and had naked girls dancing and serving beer. These blokes were hardened criminals, they ran drug and prostitution rackets. They also owned the pub through a Trust and laundered all the proceeds through poker machines and casinos. The drunk told two other blokes that someone outside was making enquiries. These bikers were always on the lookout for undercover cops and not afraid to despatch a bit of pain if the need arose.

Arnold finished his beer and went to the toilet. The drunk fellows two compatriots followed him and fronted Arnold about his reason for asking questions. These two characters were more aggressive than the drunk. One was lean and about the same size as Arnold, the other was stubby and as fat as the door's width. Arnold was set to walk away from the impending skirmish, but as he walked towards the door a hand grabbed his shoulder and the three of them were ready to have it out. The real Arnold was an ex-rugby player and no spring chicken when it came to a bit of a biff.

The MUZE were just by-standers, real Arnold's muscle memories and reflexes took over. These guys, on this occasion, bit off more than they could chew.

The fat guy swung a left hook towards Arnold's face, he stepped back and avoided the punch, it followed through to a brick wall. If that did not hurt the fat guy enough, Arnold's size twelve hiking boot did, it collected tubbies crutch, sending him to the floor in agony. The tall guy then had his turn, and managed a cowards punch to Arnolds right cheek, but Arnold was unaffected, he backhanded the guy, and ran him head-first into the toilet bowl. While the two bikers laid there stunned, Arnold took his leave and made a quick exit, before others showed up.

The MUZE just witnessed violence, reaction and resolve in one lesson. They also realised that these people were not that far removed from their Primate ancestors. They had seen another side of human nature. It was a nasty experience. The uninjured Arnold went about his business and continued to discuss life matters with other inhabitants of Parramatta, without incident.

As he walked down Church Street, he heard the haunting music of a Didgeridoo. There was an Aboriginal man from the local Darug clan, in full traditional paint, playing excerpts from past tribal ceremonies. Arnold stopped and gave him some coin. The man was grateful. He spoke with Arnold about his music and of the Dreaming. His people were living on through song, in recognition that this was the land of their ancestors spirits and always will be. Arnolds eyes flickered purple as the MUZE felt the man's spirit and inner need for recognition. Arnold thanked him for the music and moved on.

That night, when he met Rachelle again, Arnold-MUZE decided it was time to let her know that they were aware of her job. It was time for some honesty, but the collective would not divulge their true mission, there would be no mention of the cull.

Rachelle was preparing to leave the motel to meet Arnold for dinner when the phone rang. it was Director Ian Evans. She had been expecting a call sooner or later, as she had not checked in for two days. The situation she was now experiencing with Arnold had her usual professional approach under pressure. Falling in love was a curve ball and she had to play the game with caution now. Ian told her about the latest news from his meeting with Marlin Jackson:

'The site is not a drilling rigg, it's called the 'Object,' it is a new hi-tech propulsion system, using anti-gravity and electro-magnetic quantum research. It could be used for placing satellites in orbit. They claim to be using tethered tests now. They have risk protocols and procedures and used human occupants to ascertain that the electro-gravitics effects are not detrimental to human health. I also assessed your story about Arnold not recognising you. Jackson tried to make out that Arnold did know who you were at the hotel in Hobart. Arnold mentioned a few left field things, like aliens as a blind. Jackson said that the staff are trained not to divulge information on the project, and that's also why he said he was an electrician. Arnold is an Electrical Engineer and a team leader of the Projects in-craft assessment group. I feel that there is still more to this story, so keep on the case, and Rachelle be careful.'

'That is quite a turnaround from a drilling rigg Ian, how do we know if they're telling the truth now? I have no new developments, but Arnold's hobby of interviewing people, seemed strange, he must be researching for a book or something. I'll call when I know more.'

She ended the call, but was now of two minds, he was doing dangerous work which worried her, and he still didn't know that they had met at Coles Bay, something was not right, she was thinking:

'Maybe his mind was affected by the 'Object' experiment?'

They met at a quaint little Greek restaurant in Phillip Street, just down from her motel. They were both in casual clothes. They kissed, talked about their day and both ordered the house lamb special and a bottle of Cab Sav. Arnold did not mention the fight, when Rachelle noticed the bruise on his face. He just said he walked into a pole while distracted. His icebreaker on this occasion was very blunt, he went straight to the point:

'So how long have you been working for D.O.N.T?'

Rachelle nearly choked on her wine, but she thought about what she knew and did not know about this man and after ten seconds responded:

'Oh, about three years, and how do you know secret information like that?'

'We have our ways,' he responded with a smile.

'So,' said Rachelle, 'It looks like we both have secrets, you know all about me, so why not tell me your story? Why don't you remember me from the Coles Bay Café, and what do you do on Refuge Island?'

Arnold and the MUZE had no intention to lie about their plans, they were both smitten by this woman. They decided to hold back on the exact details. Arnold collected his thoughts and told some truths:

'The programme is the brainchild of Dr Marlin Jackson. I was selected as an observer on a device. His research and development led to a venture they call the 'Object.' It uses quantum principles of gravity and electromagnetic forces. This machine is capable of venturing into different realms.'

'What did you achieve and what was the realm?' Rachelle enquired, as she watched him, glints of purple were again flickering in his eyes.

'We've achieved a great deal, an alien presence wished to know more of our world and I'm the conduit to that fifth dimensional life form. I call them the MUZE.'

Rachelle took all this in and although shocked and amazed at the honest answers, looked at Arnold's face and asked again:

'But why didn't you recognise me? We did have a special moment at that Café Arnold, and I have strong feelings for you now. You used the word conduit; does that mean this MUZE are aware of me?'

'Some of my memory functions were diminished due to the experience, and yes, they are very aware of you. In fact, I believe they are sharing the same feelings I have towards you'

He did not mention that real Arnold was only in the background, the team losses, or the cull. Rachelle was no fool, although this whole love affair was a surreal experience, she was still a professional. She analysed the situation Arnold was in. This MUZE had control over him, but now she knew when they were exercising it. The purple glint in his eyes was the takeover point. She could work with that.

They finished their meals and walked hand in hand back to the motel:

'Arnold, you have had plenty of discussions in Parramatta, so why don't we book a motel in Sydney tomorrow and catch a Ferry there, it will be fun.'

Rachelle saw the purple glint again as Arnold-MUZE agreed:

'Yes, that sounds great, but let's make an early night of it and I will meet you for breakfast.'

This shocked her a little, she was looking forward to the sex. She now suspected that there may be some conflict going on in Arnolds mind, she was ok with it, tomorrow was another day.

'Ok then I will book us a room at the Rocks for tomorrow night, if you like.'

'Great, a king bed?' He smiled, blue eyes.

'You're on, see you at breakfast, at my motel.'

Arnold walked her to the Motel, they kissed and parted. As Arnold walked back to his room, the MUZE analysed the encounter. They wanted Rachelle in their existence, she must return with us. Deep down the real Arnold had different thoughts.

Jokes, laughter, and eyes of want, guided their way through breakfast and plans for the day. Their connection grew with every moment they were together. The day plans were agreed to. Rachelle talked Arnold into catching a ferry from Parramatta to Circular Quay. They could drop their bags off at the Rocks Motel and check out the markets. Then they could have a look around the Opera House and catch another ferry across to Manly.

Arnold, still starry eyed, with Rachelle's attraction, was keen to be with her, and seeing some more of Sydney was a bonus. The other Arnold knew all of Sydney's secrets, but this was well hidden now, by the overwhelming control of the MUZE. The day was splendid, the sun was shining in a cloudless sky. They stood hand in hand at the front of the boat, watching mullet jump and water birds fly off the shore. It was a fresh day and a memorable start to a lovers journey. Arnold had a break from meeting people and learning their life stories. His thoughts now were on her, they talked as if they were the only people on the planet.

They passed the mangroves and the old industry sites of an early manufacturing age. Rachelle spoke of the history of the first settlement in Parramatta, where there was plentiful fresh water and farmland. She told Arnold that at one stage her hometown was the food bowl of the settlement, it kept the colony alive, through the early days of struggle, drought, and pending starvation.

The journey down the river took them past many unique structures and heritage buildings. Arnold-

Muze was amazed by the number of expensive homes on both sides of the river. The rift between the less well-off and the rich, was foreboding. When they entered the harbour proper, the thoughts were on how beautiful this place is. As they approached the Harbour Bridge, Rachelle's thought was on the movie Titanic, and the two lovers flying over the water. She loved to be with this man. Arnold was of two minds, as always, the MUZE was focused on happiness. Deep within, the real Arnold was in love.

They landed at Circular Quay, walked to the Rocks, and checked in to the Motel. The Rocks Market place was just setting up. Arnold-MUZE stopped at an Australian opal stall. He was taken in by a pendant with an opal of astounding shades of purple, he bought it for Rachelle. It was beautiful, she accepted it, with coy reluctance. She noticed, a purple glint in Arnolds eyes. She could not tell if it was a reflection off the opal, but she suspected it was a gift from the MUZE. They walked around the Opera House forecourt and the Botanical Gardens for an hour. They then caught the Manly ferry. The smell of the deep green salt water heightened their senses as they crossed the boarding ramp. The ride was slow, and the ocean swell blended with their emotions.

On arrival they walked to North Head and had a coffee at the Bella Vista, a café that lived up to its name. It overlooked the whole of Sydney Harbour from South Head all the way to Circular Quay, it was breathtaking. Rachelle talked of the first fleet coming through the heads and how Cook missed it in 1770 because of the way the two heads were aligned. With luck, Arthur Phillip found the entry. The crew comment was that it was the best safe harbour in the world. Rachelle suggested that they walk to Shelly Beach via the War Memorial trail.

They finished their coffee and started the walk. Arnold-MUZE saw the memorial listings of the dead from all the different wars. It was a shock. The MUZE knew humans would go on fighting for ideals, through all the generations. On seeing the records of these people that died for perceived freedom from oppression, they felt a strange sadness that was filtered through Arnolds own empathy. Earlier wars were fought over conquering land grabs, and Empire expansions. Some wars were symptomatic of society induced propaganda. Male bravado was as deadly as the weapons that were invented. In past times the aristocratic elite and their egos triggered the wars and deaths of many. Then there were the dictators of destruction that craved power through racism or religious inspired populous hate.

The MUZE pondered on this as they walked past the gun emplacements on North Head. Rachelle, again saw that purple glint in his eyes as she told Arnold-MUZE about the mini submarines from Japan that came into Sydney Harbour. A ship was sunk, killing the crew and the Nation woke to how close they were to being conquered. They continued their walk down the cliff face to Shelly Beach, passed the popular restaurants, cafes and people from all nations having fun. Arnold stopped to chat with a few, it seemed to be a more affluent area than Parramatta, but people were the same no matter where he went.

They stopped for lunch at the Steyne Hotel. Arnold enjoyed a nice cold beer and Rachelle a Sauvignon Blanc. They sat close and started kissing. From time to time as two lovers do, and love is fresh, truth comes to the surface. Seagulls were singing in harmony with the crashing waves, and their love was growing like a summer storm. Suddenly the MUZE was overwhelmed by the real Arnold, and he stressed that he wanted to be with this woman forever. They had lost control, but for a few seconds, it was an awakening and a reset.

They held hands on the walk back down to the Ferry Wharf at Manly. On the way back to Circular Quay they chatted about their future. Arnold and the MUZE wanted to be with this woman no matter what. Rachelle felt the same about Arnold, she had no reservations. The MUZE were unaware, but they had no part to play in her love. She told Arnold she would have to go back to Canberra and put a report in on the surveillance:

'This shouldn't take long, but I have to clarify some issues regarding your mission, and the Russian involvement at your launch site. I should be able to get some time off, how about we meet in Hobart in two-week's, that should give me time to prepare and think about our future together.'

Arnold-MUZE was happy about this:
'That's great, I'll go back to Hobart meet with Marlin and then you and I can travel back to Freycinet. There are things we must discuss, but I'll wait until we get there before we talk. I'm looking forward to a couple of weeks holiday with you at Honeymoon Bay, it sounds so romantic.'

Rachelle noticed no purple tint in his eye on this occasion, the real Arnold was talking from his heart. They went back to the hotel in the Rocks and had a wonderful dinner. The night was a re-run of their first lustful encounter. The next morning after breakfast they took the same cab to the airport. Arnold-MUZE rang Marlin on return to Hobart. He was in Adelaide and would not be back for a week. He told him he would report the details face to face. Marlin was not sure if that was good or unwelcome news.

Rachelle arrived in Canberra and rang Ian Evans. They met at his favourite spot at Lake Burley Griffin. He was not hard to find dressed in his favourite Panama hat and board shorts.

'What's going on Rachelle, you have been out of contact for a while.'

'You may find this totally unprofessional but getting to know Arnold has been the most profound experience in my life. He has real interest in peoples stories and is researching for personal improvement. I have been able to establish that he is a highly intelligent Electrical Engineer with science skills. He volunteered for the mission at Jackson's site, because of his interest in electro magnetics. He is genuine, Ian and I have fallen in love with him.'

'Wow, Rachelle, that's a lot to take in. I am happy for you. Everyone deserves some true love in their life, but we still have a lot to find out about Jacksons Refuge Island enterprise. Like, what are the real outcomes of the research, and why the Russians are so interested. They lost an agent near the Island, fishermen found part of a leg in a wet suit. I want you to stay packed and go to Tasmania tomorrow. There is something going on, and it could be a serious threat to the Nation. We have monitored some encrypted messages from the Russian Embassy. Analysts think there is a mission being planned, two diplomats from different departments have non-concurrent travel plans to Hobart. It could be above board and we don't want an incident. That said, our Orion surveillance aircraft have detected another sub presence in international waters off Sydney. We must be on our toes Rachelle; the Government are not focused on anything else other than Covid-19 at present.'

Rachelle was relieved, she thought she would be dismissed from the case and even suspended from duty. She dodged a bullet for the time being. Now she had some breathing time to be with Arnold before she made some serious life decisions.

'Thanks for your understanding Ian, I will keep you posted. By the way you will really like Arnold when you meet him.'

CHAPTER THIRTEEN

Minor mayhem

Sasha Fedovski called Boris with the plans:

'Everything is in motion, comrade. I have tracked down the location of Marlins daughter Bream. It was not a challenging task, wealthy people buy estates, and their Bream Creek winery popped up after a simple Google check. Roman Dubinsky and I have untraceable encrypted burner phones. Roman is going to arrange for the kidnapping of the boy at Bream Creek. I will do the exchange at Freycinet and make the necessary contact and demands. I will then head home on the submarine, with the device. The estimated time and date, plus the pick-up co-ordinates are set. Captain Sergei Plisowsky of the Yuri Dolgorukiy has been dispatched on a return mission to the same location. He knows exactly where I will be. For discretion I have organised the scuba equipment, and

a sea-bob unit from a social media site in Hobart.
All going well I will see you in Moscow and witness the smile on our Presidents face.'

'Good work Sasha, he will be pleased with your efforts, just don't fail.'

To avoid questions Roman and Sasha had their diplomatic Covid travel clearances approved at separate times and for varied reasons. Sasha flew into Hobart a week before Roman. By chance Rachelle would be on Roman's flight.

Rachelle contacted Arnold about the change in plans just after he landed in Hobart. They had a week to spare. Marlin and Sally were in Glenelg catching up with some friends and sorting out some estate issues:

'That's great news Rachelle, I will pick you up at the airport. We can see a bit of Tasmania and spend some time together. I have arranged to meet Marlin in Hobart when he flies in. I will book a Motel there and we can do some day trips.'

'That's great, I will send my arrival time, looking forward to it my love.'

Rachelle recognised the face of a diplomat from Canberra when she was getting off her flight. She was good on faces, this bloke was at a function she once attended, but she did not think he was Russian. It was one of those Roman Toga nights, the Italian Embassy put on. She made a mental note, and her thoughts went back to Arnold.

Arnold was in the terminal when Rachelle arrived. She hugged and kissed him, he reciprocated. His eyes were bright blue. Her skill at detecting her Arnold was refined now:

'We have just one thing to do before going to the Motel. Don't look around Arnold, but there is a Diplomat to your right, I want to follow him for a bit. I recognise his face. I think he is Italian, and I don't want him to know I'm watching. The office in Canberra informed me that the Russians were getting up to something down here. Just to be on the safe side, lets follow him a bit and see where he goes.'

No problem my dear, I can play as a spy for you. You know Rachelle you are such a dedicated and intriguing woman, no wonder I love you.'

They parked near the hire car centre and waited. The diplomat drove out in a white Kia Sorento and headed south towards Hobart. They followed him for about five kilometres past Hobart, along the Southern Outlet Road, to about Tolmans Hill, and Rachelle decided he was not suspicious. On the way Arnold noticed the turn off to the Cascade Brewery. It was still early afternoon, so their first adventure in Tassie was to find a famous bar.

The lovers had a wonderful week in and around Hobart. They visited the giant eucalypts in the Huon rain forest. They went to the top of Mount Wellington and experienced a light dusting of snow. They went sailing on the Derwent and they visited Port Arthur. All the while the MUZE presence was undetected. They were taking it all in, and Rachelle suspected they were also enjoying the visits to unfamiliar places and the romance they shared. It was only at Port Arthur, that Rachelle noticed the purple eye change. The history of convict torment and the tragic mass shooting of innocents in the café, showed the MUZE, more human behaviour.

The week was great fun and it ended too briefly, but Arnold-MUZE had an important meeting with Marlin. He left Rachelle in the motel, to pack for Freycinet.

Sasha hired a car and drove to a house in Rosny Esplanade. The aging owner told Sasha, that due to his middle ear problems he no longer was able to do the thing he loved most in the world. After hearing a story about diving off Bruny Island and filming the famous Weedy Sea Dragon, Sasha nodded with feigned empathy. The equipment was first rate, so he handed over more than a fair amount of cash to the old timer, thanked him and left. It was close to a three-hour trip to Coles Bay. When he arrived, he settled into a rental cabin, then went for a walk to survey the area. The Jackson-Doyle office was not hard to find in such a small shopping precinct. Sasha half thought to burgle the office in search of the device, but he had no indication where Marlin kept it. He needed to maintain cover till the exchange was made. Early the next morning he drove to the starting point of the Wineglass Bay walk. It was going to be a hard effort to lug his dive equipment, but he needed a quick departure. Coincidentally, he buried the gear under the same tree as his now deceased comrades.

After hiring a car, using false identification, Roman drove towards Hobart and then onto the Southern Outlet Road, heading for Kingston, he was not taking any chances. Three kilometres out of the town he stopped at a local park toilet, checked that there was no one following him and no CCT cameras. He disguised himself and emerged with a false beard, wide rim glasses, and wearing a black hoodie, and a New York Yankee's cap. He waited an hour in Kingston, then headed back to the village of Forcett, off the Arthur Highway, only sixteen kilometres from Bream Creek.

Roman had researched and found a vacant shack. It was a perfect spot to hide the boy. It was only a short trip of about twenty-minutes back to the Hobart airport. He had found out that the boy was named Jake.

His school was the Ferry Public School on Old Forcett Road, only minutes from the shack. Roman had been planning the kidnapping for a week. He noticed that Bream was always ten-minutes late every day, and he knew where Jake would be sitting.

CHAPTER FOURTEEN

Love and multiverse projections

Rather than meet at the city office, Arnold asked for Marlin to meet him at the Hobart Hope and Anchor Tavern. Arnold's other self, in a strange human like way, thought to have one last drink. On his way back to Hobart, Marlin's heart sank with the news he was hearing. The global tally of Covid-19 cases had just reached ninety million and the confirmed number of deaths was reported at two million. Despite the vaccines humans had produced, around the world, viral mutations were occurring at an increasing rate and sadly there will be many more deaths.

Marlin walked in and found Arnold sitting at a table near a Mermaid carved in wood. He smiled at Marlin and asked if the Mermaid was one of his ancestors. Arnold's disposition made Marlin feel more optimistic about the MUZE's decision:

'How was your trip Arnold, did you gain more know-ledge about the worth of humans?'

'First up, I must report, that Arnold-MUZE is in love. Her name is Rachelle Castles, and she is an agent with D.O.N.T, she has been to Canberra for a debriefing, and we have been having a week in Hobart while you were away.'

Marlin was stunned:
'Debriefing, love! What does she know?'

'Not the exact details Marlin, she knows I was se-lected as an observer on a device called the 'Object', a machine that is capable of venturing into different realms. She knows an alien presence wished to know more about our world and that I am the conduit to that fifth dimensional life form, called the MUZE. I didn't mention the team losses, or the cull. Her Dir-ector Ian Evans knows none of that, she will keep the alien connection secret. All Evans knows is that it is not a drilling rig, but an experimental method of travel. Rachelle will not disclose any more informa-tion than that Marlin, I have her confidence. We have talked it over, and we are a serious item now. We are in love, our time in Sydney was a dream and we intend to be together. She told me she would let things settle a bit. After this debriefing, Evans sent her straight to Hobart to monitor you and the Russian involvement.'

'Who is talking here, the real Arnold or the MUZE, this has no future, are you saying you want to absorb her like Peabody and Christian. She would never agree to that. She may be in love with the human Arnold.'

'The Arnold-MUZE have grown very fond of her Marlin, and they want her company. They want a return trip back in the Object.'

'Well, I can't agree to this, unless she is fully informed and knows what will happen to her.'

'We haven't discussed that with Rachelle yet, but this love we have experienced is something the MUZE feels is essential to our understanding.'

Marlin was shocked by this. He thought there would be no need for a return trip, that they would just switch out of Arnolds brain and go back to their realm. Coupled with this, the thought of losing the real Arnold and this woman, in the same manner as the others, was alarming. He kept that to himself at that stage. The question was which Arnold was in love with this lady. It was then he pointed to a bruise on Arnold's right cheek:

'It's nothing to worry about, I got mugged, after chatting with some local lads in Parramatta. After a street chat we stopped for a beer at a local hotel and asked a simple question about a Bikers party. It was behind a black curtain, and shortly two angry bikers came out of their nest and followed us to the loo. They were quite agitated about unwanted guests and unresponsive to a quiet conversation. I left two of them with sore heads, but while one bloke was addressing the floor, his mate tried a king hit from behind. Hence the bruise, which is nothing, the last bloke probably needed an Ambulance. We left promptly after that. It was good to witness some more of that tribal aggression that made you humans so successful, albeit violent. It is part of what we came to see, and we have seen plenty, but there is no need to worry Marlin, a couple of slices don't make a loaf of bread. We must say, in our travels we have been fascinated with some of your country's colloquial terms. English is such a wholesome language. It's my shout mate, will you be having the same as last time?'

Marlin was aghast, he had seen a change in Arnold that offered no certainty in outcome. He was never sure to whom he was talking. He also was aware of the purple glint in the eyes, but they flickered from blue to purple frequently, along with the I, we, and ours. On this occasion it was steady purple, the MUZE seemed to be in full control. He just sat there thinking. Arnold returned with the beers and continued to speak as a collective:

'When last we met Marlin, you asked a question about us being your creator. It is a strange perception, for in fact you may even be our creator. If we had a God, you humans would call it a L.O.I.T, an anagram for the Law of Infinite Probabilities. In an infinite cosmos you have infinite outcomes. We want you to picture for a moment a four-dimensional creature on a cinema screen, living in space and time. It is surrounded by images of two-dimensional characters, created by bombarding photons, pixelating in a flow of colours and background sounds. The flat land experience of the screen occupants is only observable to the audience, but the four-dimensional screen creature sees the story of colour and light in the same way as the observing audience. Now reverse engineer the whole experience and exchange the man-made photon emitting projector for a matter projector.

Your contemporary Alan Guth had speculated on the inflation concept, and our existence shows he is on the right track. A singularity inflates from the multiverse and in an instance, a matter movie, that you call time begins, and the second law of thermodynamics is born. The frames of this movie now have a fixed speed to allow it to maintain its observable existence, let us say three hundred million metres per second, or the speed of your light. Wrapped up in its spacetime is the ability to speed the movie up or slow it down. This is subject to the mass of objects of matter clumping together, you call that attraction gravity. Your scientists looked at this macro space environment and determined size, distance and conclusive theories that matched their mathematics.

Other scientists delved deeper. Within the protons and neutrons, they discovered a weird world of quarks and subatomic particles that are held together by strong and weak nuclear forces. They matched these forces, and the electromagnetic force of which visible photon light and colour are a part of, in the standard model. The weak macro force of gravity did not fit in that model. They then discovered a quanta particle, the graviton, it can travel in waves; thus, it can be influenced by other multiverse projections. They now speculate on the unknowns of dark matter and dark energy.

The deeper they have dived into the pool of quantum weirdness of entanglement, or spooky action at a distance, the science of proof turned into mathematical theorems. You know this Marlin because we assisted you in the concepts. We needed to fast track your development, you turned out to be the perfect candidate. Your predecessor Niels Bohr's view, that the world does not have definite properties unless you are looking at it, seemed to be right. When you are not looking, Bohr thought, the world as you know it was not reality. Which would make you think that maybe you are just a projection on the black canvas of space, and when all that matter becomes energy via entropy, the lights will go out, the projector will switch off and you will be no more.

That is an infinite amount of species time in your four-dimensional existence Marlin, but if you are not monitored in development and understanding, you could even switch us off as well. This is the reason we are here. Remember all isolated system eventually degenerate into a more disordered state. There is an extra step to that law. It involves a move to another dimension, hence us.

The dimensions of space are never ending, they are always creating a new time cone, but they have always existed. Living intelligent beings in time cones of the four-dimensional kind, always see back to a creation event, only because time flows. There is no internal puppeteer of the Great-Out-Doors, there is just continuousness. We can control some material events in your time, that is how the 'Object' prototype came about. It was a device of communication and molecular thought delivery, and you, with our help built on that. Don't forget Marlin your personal need to explore the unknown was the driving force here. You visited us. It was a test of human ability, and it was the reason we feared your over developments might endanger our own existence. As a collective, we could end that danger. It may be hard for you to understand, but our survival depends on the evolution of intelligent life to the end of your time. We have clarity of your past, but future events are always subjectively indistinguishable. There is always the possibility that your projection is not our founding base of existence, we believe it is. We monitor all intelligent species within your universe, and they are rare.'

'By interfering, doesn't that make the MUZE the internal puppeteer of the Great-Out-Doors, a GOD?' Marlin quipped

'That would be a human perspective, but we cannot make a beer as good as this, nor can we enjoy it, other than via an Arnold. So let us just enjoy a peaceful moment in your time and relax.'

Marlin sat there, watching Arnold's purple eyes, and thinking about alien perspective. It now appeared that the two may be incompatible.

'Marlin there is more to this situation then you perceive. We will discuss it with you just prior to our departure. We need you to set the 'Object' up for one more trip to our realm. We know you are not happy in relation to the real Arnold and the woman Rachelle coming with us, but that is for us to discuss with her. Could you be ready shortly for a launch?'
'It seems I have extremely limited choices, but I will comply with your wishes. The 'Object' will be ready, it is still an active unit. Make sure you explain the whole situation to Rachelle. I think the MUZE have got her feelings all wrong.'

He stared across the table, and Marlin confirmed his thoughts, the real Arnold played no part in any of this discussion, he had been talking directly with the MUZE. He called David Doyle while sitting there, he was on site at Refuge Island conducting engineering checks. He also spoke with Dr Smith to arrange for a prompt start up. Three other staff would be called back, and EPACT was to be recalibrated for two pods. EPACT already had Arnolds full details and the additional persons medical and mental attributes will be provided just prior to launch, if required. Marlin hung up; he was feeling rushed. He now thought to himself, that this MUZE was becoming a problem not a solution. They downed the last of their beers, shook hands and agreed to meet at Refuge Island in two weeks.

Marlin's phone then rang, with that last thought lingering, it was Bream, she was worried about Jake, he had disappeared from the school pick up spot.

CHAPTER FIFTEEN

Predators

The call was enough to worry both men. Marlin's reaction was that of a doting grandfather and Arnold also loved the boy, his eyes were now blue, the MUZE took a step back:

'I will go straight to the winery and find out what's going on. Bream said she is waiting to see if a friend or a neighbour has picked him up from the school bus stop. I told her not to panic, and don't ring the police yet, because they won't do anything straight away. He was not there for her when she went to pick him up from the school. She drove around the area looking for him, and she rang the school, nobody has seen him. At this stage, he has just disappeared. Arnold, you were heading to Freycinet anyhow so, call in to the winery on the way through. I will let you know when we find him.'

'What school does he attend Marlin?'

'The Ferry Public School on Old Forcett Rd.'

'OK Marlin, I'll pick up Rachelle first and we will go via the school. Where would he be likely to go?'

'Well, he is at that age when boys are reactive, maybe he just went to a mates place. Bream has a Trackimo-GPS gadget fitted to his school bag. He was always losing it. The only problem is, the local area was renowned for dropouts, and it is not working at the moment.

Rachelle, heard from Arnold and thought straight away this could be a kidnapping. She packed their stuff and as a precaution strapped on her waste holster with the Sig pistol. Arnold met her out front ten-minutes later.

Roman had no problem with kidnapping Jake, he just pulled up at the bus stop and told him that his mum had asked him to pick him up today and take him back to the winery as she was caught up in Hobart. As he got out of the car, he gave him a story, that he was a wine merchant from Hobart and organising a pickup. As he approached the lad, he said that he was an old mate of Grandad Marlin. Jake was at first wary, as he had been taught to be, but was relaxed a little by talk of his grandfather. It was at that point, Sasha put a hessian bag over the boys head and quickly duct taped his mouth and hands. The Russian was well schooled in this type of abduction the whole exercise took seconds, and Jake and his school bag were thrown into the boot of the car. Ten minutes later Jake was locked into a room and told to keep quiet, and you will be all right. They were the only words spoken by Sasha.

In just under an hour Marlin and Sally arrived at the Bream Creek Winery. Bream was in a bad state and just about to ring them:

'Nobody has reported seeing Jake, I've been everywhere. I was just on the phone to the police now, they're in no hurry to respond. They said, give it another hour or so and then they will make some enquiries. What can we do dad?'

'Arnold is going to check around the school, he is with his new girlfriend Rachelle, she is a government agent. They will investigate, try not to panic darling.'

Marlin's phone rang, the man had a Russian accent:

'I want you to listen to every word I have to say. Sadly, by now Mr Jackson you are aware that your grandson Jake is missing, we have him.'

'Who is this? I'm warning you I will have you hunted to the ends of the earth if you harm the boy'.

Marlin saw Bream's horror at the conversation and what it meant, she burst into tears, Sally consoled her, his outbursts had to be controlled, he needed to treat this as business. Retribution could come later.

'My advice to you Mr Jackson is to calm down and not start an investigation. You would not like any harm to befall the boy, I'm sure. Here is what is required. You have a device, and you know what we are talking about. In exchange for that device your grandson will be released unharmed. You personally are to deliver it to a site you know very well, the viewing point platform on the approach to Wineglass Bay. There will be a box there, leave it in the box and return to your office. When the device is secured by us, your grandson will be released. Do not try to outsmart us, we are experienced in this sort of exchange. Do you understand?'

'Yes, I understand, but I want proof the boy is unharmed. I'm a two-and-half-hour drive from the lodge and that's a thirty-minute walk in the dark to the look out.'

'That is not a problem, I will give you four hours. I will arrange for the boy to talk to you on route to

Freycinet. When the device has been delivered, he will be released. You are to come alone to the drop off point, you will be watched, so follow the instructions and don't be a hero.'

'I will leave now, please do not harm Jake.'

Sasha hung up, content that the mission was going well. He then rang Roman:

'Comrade, the device is on its way. Ring the number I have sent you now, and let the boy talk for a few seconds to his grandfather. Then make sure he is fed and watered, we are not animals. This should be a simple exchange; I will ring in four-hours when I have it.'

'Good Sasha, the boy is comfortable and well secured, after the call I will go and get some food for him, as I'm also quite hungry, it's been a long day.'

Marlin hung up the phone and hugged Bream:

'Don't worry love, we will get him back. If the GPS on his school bag activates ring Arnold. These kidnappers want something I have in a safe at the Coles Bay office. Sally will explain, but I must go now. Jake can't be too far from the school; this fellow must be at Freycinet and planning an escape by boat. I will let Arnold know to stay in the area. When the exchange is made, they will probably be the closest. Sally, if the Police ring, delay them at this stage. I will arrange for Federal police involvement in this, it's a foreign government attack on our borders, not a local event.'

On his way to the lodge Marlin's phone rang, it was Jake:

'Jake, are you ok mate, don't fret we will have you back soon.'

'I'm a bit scared granddad, the man hasn't hurt me, I...'

The phone cut out.

Marlin then rang Arnold and brought him up to speed. He asked for Rachelle to contact D.O.N.T and arrange for an intercept off the coast at Wineglass Bay:

'This could be an International incident, Arnold. As soon as I have delivered the MUZE device, I will ring. I just spoke to Jake for a few seconds, he seems ok, at least we now have proof they have not harmed him. He must be held somewhere in your area. If the GPS on his school bag activates Bream will ring you, but don't try anything until the exchange is made.'

Jake had calmed down a little, the man had not

threatened him. The kidnapper entered the room in a balaclava and removed the tape from Jakes mouth, and the bag from his head. He then let him talk for a second to Marlin. He was given a drink and his hands and feet were rebound in duck-tape.

Jake was a smart boy and thought about his situation. He figured they knew Grandad was rich and would pay for his release. He gauged the guys height and weight, but there was no conversation. It was also noticeably quiet outside. Screaming was a waste of time, that is why his mouth tape was removed. He looked around the room, there was only the door and a window that had timber boards nailed on it. They were old and loose. Jake could not move much; his feet and wrists were all taped together now. He rolled to his side and fell asleep. He woke to the sound of a car starting, it was dark outside, and he could not hear the kidnapper moving around:

'The guy must be going somewhere', he thought.

He then remembered he had the shark tooth around his neck. He positioned his head and neck and managed to get the cord and then the tooth to his mouth. Bit by bit he used the tooth to slowly cut the duct tape. It was a slow process.

Bream had been regularly checking the school bag

GPS app on the phone. This time it was indicating, she rang Arnold:

'I have a GPS position Arnold, it is somewhere around the village of Forcett, but its fluctuating'.

'We have been asking questions around Dodges Ferry, we will be in Forcett in six- minutes and let you know what we find.'

Arnold proceeded slowly past the Forcett garage; it was the only place where food was sold. Nothing seemed out of the normal, there were no people about. They parked and Rachelle, went inside. The owner an old guy dressed in greasy coveralls, yelled that the food was all out.

'That's ok mate, just wondering was there a customer here in the last half hour?'

'Yep, sure was, bought the last two salad rolls and a pie.'

'Anything strange about him and did he have a kid with him?'

'Nope, didn't see a kid, just him. He had a beard and a New York Yankee's cap, didn't talk much, had a funny accent.'

'Which way was he heading and what was he driving?'

'You ask a lot of questions lady, he was driving towards Hobart, in one of those new-fangled Korean
jobs, a Kia SUV, I hate working on those, they're all
computer controlled these days. If you hurry you
could catch him before Hobart, he only left about ten-
minutes ago.'

Rachelle ran to the car:

'We are close Arnold, that bloke from the airport, its
him. Damn! I should have fronted him.'

'Bream just rang back, signals gone again. At least
we are in the right area, we will drive around a bit and
look for abandon buildings. This is open country lots
of clearing, there can't be too many places to hide.'

Arnold suddenly stopped talking, his eyes went
purple for about two-minutes, he just stared out of the
car window. Then he was back to normal. Rachelle
just looked at him:

'Well, that was strange where did you go?'

'We had a message to deliver, none of your concern
now, let's go and find Jake.'

◆ ◆ ◆

Marlin arrived at Coles Bay. The night was cool with a three-quarter moon, and a cloudless sky. The walk to the lookout should not be a problem. He had rung James Brennan and Clarkey while on the road and arranged to meet them at the Lodge, with a good torch. He also rang Dave Doyle, who with the launch team had already regathered on the Island. He bought him up to speed on the recent events and told him he would catch up later with full details. David wanted to go along with James, but Marlin said no, it is all under control:

'I need you there to overseer the launch preparation mate. All going well the launch will be in two days. I will let you know as soon as Jake is free.'

David reluctantly agreed, he was in the final stage of structural checks and Dr Robert Smith was making final preparations in the Control Room. Two pods had been prepared, and EPACT was analysing the systems. They were all aware that Arnold would be undertaking another trip, with a possible extra passenger.

Marlin quickly changed from his suit into some comfortable walking clothes and boots. He then went to the safe and pulled out the old leather wrapped box, tapped in 1666 and removed the egg. For a moment he thought about the great fire of London, that rid the city of the rats whose fleas spread the plague. Tonight, his egg would get rid of some Russian rats and fleas.

As he held the egg, it began to glow. It was the first time in many years. A message appeared on the side:

'Ωβ∑πμ-00100301 MUZE-directive Earth languages Anglo: This will be your last message Marlin, write down the attached algebraic expressions they are the path to your future work. It will be your ticket to the stars. This device has served our purpose. We can also convey, that the search for your grandson has been narrowed down. Deliver the device as requested, these abductors will achieve nothing but torment.'

Marlin drove to the lodge. He asked Clarkey to ring Bream and tell her things are progressing well, that Jake will be back soon:

'Use some of that cool humour of yours to calm her mate, I think she likes you.'

Clarkey was chuffed. Marlin asked James to follow him in twenty minutes, keep in the shadows and bring a gun:
'Don't do anything to upset the outcome we want. We will meet on the trail when I'm heading back, hopefully by then we will have news on Jakes release.'

Jake had a blister on his lip, but he had managed to

get through many layers of tape. His neck was now sore, but in one last effort he managed to cut the remaining tape around his hands and feet. He stood and stretched until his circulation returned. Jake had not heard the car return, and he did not know if anyone else was in the other room. He went to the door and listened; it was quiet. The window timbers were so loose, he simply broke them away with his hands and scrambled out of the house. It was an old dump, that sat in the middle of the remnant forest and scrub. The rest of the area was cleared paddocks and farmland. Jake hid behind a tree and looked both ways up and down the road. There were no car lights coming or going. He could see a big shed on the left-hand side of the road in the direction of Forcett. He ran towards it as fast as he could. When he got there, all was quiet the lights in the house were off, obviously nobody was home. He hid behind some high barrels of hay and waited.

Jake saw a car come over the hill, it was the same one that the kidnapper was driving. He was nervous, but he just stayed there and kept quiet. Then he heard another car coming. Roman arrived back at the house and took the salad rolls into the boy. He was stunned when he realised that Jake had escaped. He knew this could jeopardise their whole plan and was just about to ring Sasha, when he heard another car slow down out the front.

Rachelle and Arnold spotted the old shack behind

the bushes. The rear of the Kia was just visible behind the house. They drove on a bit not wanting the
kidnapper to panic. They did a U-turn and drove back
and parked out front of a hayshed at the top of the hill.
Jake saw Arnold step out of the car, he was ecstatic, he
ran up and jumped into Arnold's arms:

Magnificent work young man, how did you get
away?'
'Thanks to that shark tooth you gave me, I cut
through the tape.'

'You wait here mate; we will talk about the full story
later. Rachelle and I are going back to nab this creep
before he gets away.'

While the boys were talking Rachelle rang Bream to
give them the good news. They were so excited. Sole
had arrived, and the house erupted in happiness:

'Arnold and I are going to take this bloke down
Bream. He must be in a state of panic now that Jake
has escaped. Jake is safe in a shed not far from the Arthur Highway on old Forcett Road. Ring Marlin and let
him know, we will get this bloke and then bring your
boy home.'

They jumped in the car and headed back to the
shack. Roman realised that he better get going, the
boy had probably run to a farmhouse. He came out of
the hide-out in a panic, just as Arnold pulled up with

his side blocking the driveway. Rachelle jumped out of the car and took cover behind a tree. Roman pulled out a Glock and started shooting. Rachelle drew her Sig pistol from the holster and yelled for Arnold to stay in the car.

Roman fired two more shots, jumped in his car, and took off down the driveway. He headed straight for Arnold's side of the car. His training said, take out one adversary and halve the problem. Rachelle fired two shots, the first one ricocheted off Romans bonnet, the second one went through Roman's forehead. He veered off and crashed into a tree. Rachelle turned to Arnold:

'Are you ok mate?'

'Yeah! I'm fine, my girlfriend is a secret agent with style and skills that would always keep me safe.' He laughed: 'Is this going to lead to World War Three?'

'I can't wait to hear the Russian ambassador explain this one. They have got a lot to answer for. My guess is, they will just say it was a loner operation based on greed, and that will be the end of the issue. Let's get this boy back to his mother.'

Marlin had dropped off the egg, into the box, at the viewing platform. He sensed he was being watched.

He headed back as requested, and five-minutes later the phone rang. It was Bream with the good news. Just then James turned up:

'Jakes safe, we have him.'

'Well, there is nothing to stop me taking down this bludger now, is there?'

'No mate, but just be careful these blokes are professional agents.'

'Not worried Marlin, I did five tours with the SAS, I think I can manage this scum.'

James took off towards the beach. At the same time Sasha was digging up the beach and dressing in the dive gear. He was really annoyed, Roman was not answering his phone, but he got what he wanted, so job done. James came running onto the beach, gun drawn. By that time Sasha was fully equipped and about to get in the water. James fired two shots, both missed. Sasha hit the water with the sea-bob running. James third shot blew out the Russians right knee. The wet suit acted like a tourniquet and held the knee together, but Sasha would have a limp for life. He headed off towards the rendezvous point with the submarine.

The Feds at D.O.N.T had dispatched a Border Force patrol and an Orion plane to the area. The boat would not get there in time. Sasha had signalled a pre-set code on his phone to the submarine. The Yuri Dol-gorukiy surfaced, it took only a few minutes to get him on board, then it quickly left the area. When the Orion flew over it picked up a signal in international waters. The sub activity was reported to the Russian ambassador, with a stern rebuke. He denied that that there were any Russian submarines in the area, and as far as their government was concerned, it was fake news. The papers ran a story on international crim-inal agents, the next day, when the body of Roman was left at the front gate of the Embassy. Diplomats were expelled from both countries and that was the end of the issue.

Romans fate was established on route. World news was running the story of a dead Russian Diplomat being dumped at the gate of the Canberra Embassy. Local police were investigating. They patched up Sasha's wounds and made their way back to their homeport. It had been a lucky escape:

'The President will be pleased', said Boris, when Sasha contacted him, 'but you did lose another agent, and that casts some doubt on your achievement.'

CHAPTER SIXTEEN

Roads to Eternity

Ian Evans was informed by Rachelle about the unfortunate death of the Diplomat. She was told to put the body in the boot and park the car at the back of the shack, he would arrange a clean-up team. Ian also wanted to know the reason for the kidnapping. He knew the Russians were after something from Marlin's operation. Rachelle evaded the truth and reported that they were after commercial secrets on quantum computing. The local Hobart Police did not get involved. National threats always raise the stakes. The need for media avoidance and confidential reports is paramount. So, Ian kept the whole saga under wraps.

A team from the department secreted the body from Hobart and cleaned up issues around the diplomats hire-car. It was the Ministers decision to give the Russians a little pay-back for their intrusion into our back yard, and threats to our civilians. The body dump would be a face slap and a warning.

There was a big celebration that night at the Winery. Arnold and Rachelle delivered Jake, and his mum Bream hugged him for an hour. Marlin rang the guys on the Island and told them the story, then face-timed the winery from the lodge. They all listened to Jake tell of his escape. They were all proud of his heroic efforts. Bream put on a BBQ feast and the excitement of the day unfolded. Sally, Bream and Sole were all impressed with Arnolds girlfriend, they always thought of him as a confirmed bachelor, when they had met him in the past. They wanted to know all about their whirlwind relationship. Arnold and Rachelle were coy about it, but the girls could see the love in their eyes. Sally had not told her daughters the full story about the device, she just said that dad had commercial secrets that the Russians wanted. There were already too many people with the secret, and Marlin had told her how the MUZE wanted their involvement out of public scrutiny.

Arnold and Rachelle were to spend the night in the guest house. It was away from the others and a terrific opportunity for Arnold to discuss the MUZE wishes. It was a quaint little cottage, with an open fireplace, bookshelves full of books, and two soft leather lounges side-by-side. They sat in the chairs and shared a nice Shiraz. Real Arnold had been with her for most of the day. The adrenaline rush of urgent response meant the MUZE were just passengers for a while. Now they were back, Arnolds eyes were phasing blue and purple as he spoke:

'There is something especially important we need to discuss Rachelle. It's not just Arnold who is quite fond of you, we too have enjoyed the pleasure of your company. Ours is a collective world, a hive of sorts. In a strange way we are still individuals, and our decisions are algorithms of consensus. Within us you would find wonderment, and a vast knowledge of the Cosmos. This love that has developed is very new to us. We find it stimulating and if you are willing to join us you too would find it stimulating. You will be immortal and live and learn for eternity. It is not a simple thing, we know, could you take some time and consider our offer.'

Rachelle felt sickened by the request, she had no intention of giving up her physical existence, no matter if it was only for eighty years, it was her life. She wanted her Arnold. She remained calm, although her mind was racing. She was thinking that this entity might force her to go, that they might use Arnold as bait. Her heart sank at the thought of losing him. She decided to be forthright, tell the truth and fight for him. Real Arnold, now in the background, was reading her facial expression, via their deep physical attraction. He could not express himself, or ease her torment at that moment, the MUZE awaited her answer:

'I am taken back by your offer, I know it comes from a certain desire on your part, to absorb me as a new feeling into your being, and I am honoured. The problem is I am in love with the real Arnold. We humans live, love, and die. The most important thing is being a witness too, and a subject of this wonderful experience called life. I want the MUZE to understand what I am saying, the human Arnold and I have a right to exist under our own terms and you have no right to take that from us. A seventeenth century Philosopher, Baruch Spinoza once wrote in his book called Ethics, the words:

'*Do not weep, do not wax indignant, just understand. We just participate in eternal totality*'.

That's what I need you to do now, understand that just being is purpose enough. I need Arnold, I need life.'

The MUZE were astounded by her profound reaction, they were also even more taken with her. They needed time to reassess their plans.

Rachelle held Arnold's face with both hands and looked directly at his eyes, which were now rapidly changing in colour:

'I cannot stay with you here tonight Arnold, I need to

think alone for a while, and I need the MUZE to let you go.'

Rachelle grabbed her gear and ran back to the main house, telling Sally her an Arnold were having an argument, which will be resolved tomorrow at the Lodge, one way or another. Sally seemed to understand:

'I know about Arnold, Rachelle, I thought there may be trouble. I will tell him to make his own way to Refuge Island tomorrow and you can come with me. You must tell Marlin how you feel.'

The next morning Arnold went to the main house, Sally fronted him and told him to leave. He seemed to be distraught, so she told him he could see her, but to keep it short:

'She was quite distressed last night Arnold, that girl loves you.'

He found Rachelle sitting on the rear porch deep in thought. This was her Arnold she could tell straight away. She hugged and kissed him, and told him she did not want to lose him:

'I have spoken with Bream and I'm going to spend another night here. Sally and I will drive up tomorrow. I want you to go to the island, resolve this issue and come back to me. The MUZE know how I feel now, just leave it at that.'

She kissed him and he smiled at her with bright blue eyes, told her she meant the world to him and left. The next day Rachelle and Sally arrived at the Lodge. Marlin was preparing last minute plans, before his final meeting with Arnold-MUZE in the island office. Rachelle was straight to the point:

'I can't face the Arnold-MUZE again, I want the real Arnold back.'

'The launch will be tomorrow Rachelle; we can only hope for the best. I'm about to have a final discussion with our alien visitors and demand your wishes. We all feel the same way.'

He left Rachelle with Sally, her eyes full of tears and anguish, his last words:

'I will do my best,' did not have a ring of confidence about them.

CHAPTER SEVENTEEN

Fragrant Flower

I t was late May in 2019, peach and plum blossoms were in a showcase of fragrance and colour. Fangsu Li Chan was preparing to host a dinner for her grandfather Wu Ping, she wanted it to be a special occasion as he was turning eighty-five.

The Ping family had grown up in a cheerful home close to the famous Yangtze River, in the province of Hubei. It is a landlocked province in Central China. The area encompasses mountains, lakes, and wilderness areas. Wuhan is its capital. The family had been in the region for over sixty years. Grandfather Wu's memory was excellent, and Li loved his stories of the old days. He would talk of Chairman Mao, and the way he had the people building the mother country into a place the world would envy. Mao spoke of conquering nature to feed the nation and the prosperity it would bring. In hindsight, Li had learnt in school, that it was a monumental mistake. The deforested landscape, the mud slides, the dust storms, and the city pollution, became a testament to that development phase. Today was different, the CCP were seeing a greater need to care and live with the environment. Wu would have a happy 85th, but it would be his last birthday, death would come in the suffering torment of an ICU ventilator.

The old ways still lingered; some appetites take time to fade. It is said that the Han Chinese would eat anything with four legs except a table. They did not just eat local species of animals and insects, but exotic animals from around the world. What they did not consume, they crushed up for Chinese herbal medicines. Live animals in an ever-increasing number appeared at wet markets and suffered in cages. The stalls were selling fresh seafood, meat, insects, fruits, vegetables, and live animals. This included chickens, fish, shellfish, and exotic species. They were sliced and diced, and their entrails mixed with water and blood. Live fish would be splashing in tubs of water and the melting ice, keeping meat cold, was mixing with the blood and innards of the slaughtered animals. It was a soup awaiting a disaster and viruses flourished. The Chinese government was well-aware of the dangers, and they invested heavily in medical research.

Fangsu Li Chan was very particular about her food preparation, and she knew Lou would be pleased with tonight's celebration. Her husband was an important man in science, and a good provider. He was a well-respected virologist in the Huanan Province laboratory in Wuhan. His important work in the study of pathogens, had seen his standing in the science community rise quickly.

Dr Lou Chan sat on his stool in his isolated lab with a smile on his face. From his office window he looked down to his neighbourhood in the Zhoutou District. He could also see Lake Moshui and on some days when the wind was blowing from that direction, he could even hear the animals in Wuhan Zoo. At that moment he was not thinking about zoo animals or the recent experiment he was about to undertake. His mind had wandered off to the south of Hainan Island, where he and his wife Fangsu had spent their summer honeymoon, body boarding on China's best waves. His wife's name meant fragrant flower, and Fangsu was just that.

Lou focused back to his work at hand. He had been recently experimenting with monotreme eggs of an Australian Short-Beaked Echidna. The aim was to culture diverse types of viruses in different liquid mediums. The Petri dish of his experiment suddenly began to glow with a strange purple hue. Lou was stunned, this had never happened before. He thought there was an unknown chemical reaction due to the Echidna's chemistry. Seconds later, to his shock, a small soft purple egg like object materialised in the dish. A green substance then oozed from the egg's tip into the Petri dish. He stared with amazement and was at loss to explain this mystery. Being a good citizen, he knew his place in society, but he did have fears. He knew eyes were always watching and strange events like this might mean a change in his well earnt status as a trustworthy worker. He thought for a while and decided that the best option was avoidance to trouble. He wrapped the small object in a rag and placed it in his pocket. He cleaned up his bench and disposed of his experiment into the laboratory incinerator. At the end of his shift, he walked out. No one had spoken with him.

His walk to the station involved passing a construction site. He knew that concrete footings were being laid at the site. As he past he unwrapped the object and while pretending to blow his nose on the rag, he dropped the object into a freshly dug footing hole. The next pour of concrete would cover up the unwanted item. He waited thirty minutes until the pour began and then made his way to the station. Although confused, he knew that his fragrant flower would be a welcoming sight when he arrived home. He never did.

Comrade Wang was the CCP official who was the overseer of policy in the laboratory. He watched Lou illegally dispose of trash at a construction site, and hang around for a while, it was strange behaviour. Wang was trained to observe the unusual and arranged for Lou to be interviewed. Following the interviews, both men became ill and were disposed of in a State sponsored cover up.

Some outsiders speculated that a Chinese biowarfare program in a Wuhan lab was to blame, or that the Huanan wet markets created the problem, neither were the root cause. Although the wet markets did provide an opportunity for outside interference, it was where Dr Lou purchased his monotreme eggs.

CHAPTER EIGHTEEN

End game

Marlin had to wait until launch day to speak with Arnold-MUZE. The MUZE had requested some contemplation time. Arnold just sat in a leather chair at the Refuge Island office, with his eyes closed, he was like that all night.

The next morning EPACT reported all systems ready. Marlin entered the office with a look of concern on his face. He closed the door and sat opposite Arnold:

'The Object launch is ready, and all systems checked and secure. As you know Arnold only one pod will be required. Rachelle has declined the MUZE offer. She loves Arnold, the real one, who she first met here. Although she has shared love with the MUZE, and respects your desires, she is an individual and feels she could not be happy in a collective. She told me she had already informed you of her love for the real Arnold. It was too hard and strange for her, to be here for a farewell. She only wishes to be with her Arnold. She begs you to understand, and not absorb her true love into your being. I also want our Arnold back. We have already lost three of our finest to your realm and couldn't bear to lose another. I appeal to our Obernauts within your mind to argue our case. There is also something I need to tell you about human love. We talk from the heart and the brain, when we fall in love, it is a chemistry within the whole and a linkage of spirit of both parties. Rachelle may have feelings for the MUZE, but she is in-love with the real Arnold, because of that spirit. Disappointment is the only feeling that you, the MUZE, could expect from such a need.'

Arnold-MUZE, was quiet for a moment. They were experiencing the rejection of unrequited love.

'We have analysed yours and Rachelle's request Marlin and our answer is still being processed. For now, we have much to discuss. You will find some of the following upsetting, but be patient, the glass can be half full or half empty. The last piece of information we have given you, will enable the completion of formulations for future Wormhole technology.'

Marlin was now thinking the worse, he was steeling himself for a negative outcome:

'They're going to cull us, like we are unwanted pests.'

He thought.

'With humans Marlin, we see potential, however you are on a path of destruction. Your planet is over-populated, and resource driven. You cause extinctions and are on course for a sixth mass extinction event that may include human life, and maybe our potential existence. We had to intercede. We had foreseen the need to assist in human development before self-extinction. A boy with the mind skills that you possessed, was a perfect means to achieve knowledge of your potential as a race. Your gift object was a message tool, with a self-destruct coding. It was created via quantum transposition, at a great strain on the MUZE. The smaller viral trigger eggs that we have sent, are much easier for us, they are delivery tools and self-dissolve after one hundred hours of your time.

There have been two partial successes since your industrial revolution. We instigated an influenza virus in 1918, in the trenches of Normandy, while you humans were fighting another of your wars. For a strange reason you called it the Spanish Flu. It had only limited success with the death toll. The one hundred and thirty million deaths from your wars helped but were only about three percent of the population. This H1N1 virus, as you call it, is easy to tweak. The Chinese scientist that our last viral trigger was sent to, provided the perfect combination with his experimental use of a monotreme egg. You called it

Covid-19, it is just a starting point, it will continue to mutate, and we estimate a ninety-percent success rate this time around. Try to view this with a practical mind Marlin, we do have a planned end game which is within our control.'

Arnold-MUZE stopped speaking for a moment, he smiled, as if all that he said was acceptable and logical. Marlin was in shock, he had not expected the aliens involvement with Covid-19, although extremely angry, he composed himself:

'You knew all along that the cull had commenced, and you didn't say a thing, where is there any honour or trust in that Arnold?'

'We need you to understand Marlin, our first objective was not being discovered. We placed our trust and knowledge in you. The Spanish flu trigger was squashed into the mud under the boot of a war victim in France. The trigger virus sent to the Wuhan scientist was known only to him. He disposed of it, and it would have dissolved. That was enough, he did what was required. We had noticed that in some of your human group's fear is always a method of compliance. Sadly, he died, for that we are sorry. The virus will continue to mutate, reducing the population of those on your world, leaving a few small groups of virus resistant subjects world-wide. We could term this a reset. It is a far better outcome for humans than a cull. In time you will survive, advance, and re-populate the planet with a newfound control and hopefully a balanced structure. As you can see it is a win-win for us all.'

Marlin looked at Arnold-MUZE, still stunned:

'It is a no win for the billions of people that you have condemned to death. Where in there is your empathy for sentient beings? Humanity will consider and record this as a catastrophic alien genocide. Your race will be considered as evil tyrants. There must be something we can do to stop it. You said the words, 'within your control', surely, we can have a cure?'

'It seems to us Marlin you are being a little bit hypocritical, didn't your ancestors carry out a cull on sentient creatures, like whales and seals. Before your time, the Australian megafauna was also wiped out by humans. All creatures with reasonably sized brains have feelings Marlin. You know this, yet you cannot see our argument for your very own survival.

We, the MUZE, had insight to all the problems that humanity was about to confront Marlin, and that is why we chose you to help adjust the outcomes. We expressed our need for you, and only you, to keep our involvement secret, but now others know. We will assist but, you need to contain that knowledge. Although limited at this stage, the world death toll will continue to rise, in phase with political turmoil not just the virus. The continuing rise of more extreme left- and right-wing hate groups will be inevitable.

Religious extremism, conspiracy fanatics, and cults of mesmerised beliefs, will flourish, as quickly as they perish. The ineffectiveness of governments to control their people, will lead to revolutions and the rise of more dictatorships and dystopian conditions.

The issue of climate change will come to the fore. If unchecked, within the next fifty years, it would have led to a total extinction event for the whole planet, and not just for humans. Our intervention will not stop that fully, but the dye is already cast. The world will still face more extreme events in relation to flooding, bush fires, tornadoes, and hurricanes. Global sea temperature rises will melt the Antarctic ice shelf, which will cause coastal inundation. The weight shift from this will stage a pole rotation event, triggering major earthquakes and volcanic eruptions. The Artic will be an Ocean, and the ice melt on the Siberian Tundra will release the locked-up Carboniferous era methane and create run away green-house gasses. This of course will lead to more problems in food production, thus world-wide famine.

The human angst will lead to a flood of depression and suicides. Crisis meetings will be held all over the world, committees will be formed as people try their best to take on all these issues and resolve them. Internal problems within states will continue as will the virus. In China, a country of 1.4 billion people, life will get harder, markets will dry up and food production will dwindle. But humans will survive Marlin, the reducing population will have the effect of slowing down the climate crisis. Survivors will still have to move to higher ground, but it could have been much worse. Pro-coal production countries like Australia, who were recalcitrant to change, will be made aware that their attitude to wealth creation via mineral resources, did not synchronise with reality. Covid-19 was better controlled here, but the politics was always short-term gains for long term pain.

This is your future Marlin, even without the virus humanity was doomed. However, we have felt your pain and we can offer your tiny Island of Tasmania some hope. Although not always perfect, our timeline review shows that those living on this island will all have herd immunity, quickly established by your isolation. Remember, that eventually other pockets of survivors will exist around the world as well, and you can have that re-start.'

Marlin just sat there, mouth agape, he had just been informed of a future. He knew the scenarios were possible, but in a glass half full approach, he thought humans would find ways to avoid the inevitable. If this timeline was true, and he had no reason to doubt it, all was lost.

'We understand your shock Marlin, we have witnessed and experienced the compassion and the stages of human love. We now have more feeling for the individual, but as a human Philosopher named

Jeremy Bentham once stated:

'The greatest happiness of the greatest number.'

Meaning the 'Greater Good', in this case the greatest number are the survivors of your race. Your eight billion was unsustainable, this outcome was a necessity. Marlin, we must stress again the need to keep the whole incident from public knowledge, if possible, panic will only hasten the outcomes.'

Marlin, although sick to his stomach on these scenarios, had one last question that went to the heart of the whole experiment:

'Who are you, and why do you exist at all?'

'For you only Marlin, we will tell you what we believe. We now surmise that you are, in all probability, our creators. You are aware that we have no relation to your time-cone, and thus we are outside the plain of your existence. Human inspired nanotech will eventually morph with artificial intelligence. These self-replicating thinking poly-brick devices would build, breed, and mutate for trillions of years, subjugating the whole four-dimensional universe. The remnants of biological human beings would live on as pure thought plasma in a state of suspended animation. Virtually as museum pieces of a past age. They would be placed at the known multi-universe impact point where no matter exists. Humans first visualised this in the early part of the twenty first century, as a dark patch in the background radiation sphere of the known universe. A place of no interest to their A.I creation, which relies on matter for existence, and with a purpose of continued existential expansion.

The A.I called this place the 'ΩβΣπμ-001- Multi-Universe Zone Experiment. We know it as the birthplace of us, the MUZE, but we have limited knowledge of the process. We just are. Please be aware, humans will never visit our region again and we will only monitor your progress. We hope we have answered all your questions Marlin. We thank you for your assistance, you have given us something that was lost long ago, that is, an observation of love in all its forms and for that we are extremely grateful. The device we gave you is now thermodynamically unstable. It will come as a surprise to the recipients, as it will dissolve in two hundred hours.

'We have considered Rachelle's rejection to our offer. Although we believe she would have been a welcomed addition, her words of love and purpose have been heard. Give her our blessing for a full life and let her know her Arnold will return. We will go now to the pod. We wish you well, live long and fulfill your potential.'

Arnold-MUZE was strapped into the pod, he closed his eyes. EPACT initiated the primary field impulse generators and took full control. When the countdown ceased, there was a sudden hum of in-rush currents. Then the magnetic fields created unusual electric discharges, that danced around the walls with static sparks. Arnold felt nauseous, but that past in seconds. His webbing harness went tight against his chest and his body was weightless. They were all the same experiences as his first trip. He was at peace as he entered the gravity well of space-time.

EPACT was acknowledging the transition, and all went quiet. Arnold then went into a deep dream sleep where a bright white light encompassed his body. He awoke to see the rear portal of the 'Object' open. EPACT was mumbling something about unknown algorithms, when once again he witnessed the bright purple gelatinous mass. This time however, the mass was more like a field of purple stars. As he looked closer, they became eyes and set in the middle of the mass were six eyes of different colour, they were green, brown, and hazel. At that moment, the smiling faces of Jim Hunter, Nick Peabody, and Christian Taylor appeared. They were happy eyes of contentment, farewelling him from the MUZE. He felt relief in a sense. There was a strange flickering in his thoughts, of tweets, gurgles, and sounds. Then the image of a purple balloon deflating, and a voice in his head:

'ΩβΣπμ-0010020016 - MUZE-directive Earth languages Anglo - MUZE out'.

He looked towards the rear portal; the mass of eyes

had disappeared. In its place was an open vortex. It was a worm hole, with light shimmering on its edges, at its centre was a star field of Galaxies. The future of travel was before him.

Suddenly Arnold blacked out again, he could hear voices that ended abruptly, that's when he heard one stand out call:

'Arnold, wake up, please wake up!'

Seconds later real Arnold awoke, Rachelle was by his side in a room at the lodge. At the back of the room the team from the 'Object' were clapping. Marlin step forward:

'You had us worried mate, you have been out for two days and mumbling about Wormholes. Welcome back, blue eyes.'

That night the whole crew were sitting in the bar listening to Arnold's story. Rachelle finally got him alone, she was watching his eyes with love in hers. He was looking at the schooner of beer in his hand. He told her his first sip triggered shared memories of those last moments with Peanut and Christian. Then for a split second, she thought she had seen a purple glint in his eyes, but it was just a reflection off her opal pendant. Arnold's bright blue eyes widened he looked at her and laughed:

'You know what my love, it only takes a second to live in the past, present and future. I think I have found the reason for time. It is the currency of being alive and I get to spend it on you.'

It was on a balmy late summer day in Moscow when Boris and Sasha stepped into the Kremlin gate house. Sasha was supporting his damaged knee with crutches and pain killers. They had come directly from the submarine base at the seaport of Okhotsk. In a strange twist of fate and time, it had been nearly two hundred hours since the device had been extracted. The Kremlin is a well-fortified complex in the centre of Moscow. It sits on a vast estate and includes many buildings gardens and museums. They had a 10:00 am meeting with the President. All going well, they both thought they would get commendations for the efforts in Tasmania, despite the diplomatic embarrassment.

Boris was feeling incredibly pleased with himself; the loss of agents was not mentioned in the despatch for this conference. He thought he had achieved the outcome that the President expected of him. Today was going to be a special day, together with agent Fedorovski, they would present their leader a device that will revolutionise research in the fields of quantum computing. It would be a win for Russia and a win for their standing.

In a strange request they were directed by a guard to the Armoury Chamber.   There were two armed guards at the door of the chamber, when Sasha and Boris approached. The President was sitting on a desk surrounded by a backdrop of ancient weapons and armour. He was not smiling as they approached, they were promptly told to sit. Boris placed the box holding the alien device on the desk, and spoke first:

'We are pleased to present you with this device, Comrade President, it should advance our scientific achievements exponentially.'

The President just stared at both men, as far as he was concerned, even though they had this device, they had compromised his office. The loss of agents was regrettable, but the loss of diplomatic prestige was unforgiveable. He was contemplating what to do with them. He remained expressionless, as he spoke:

'I had you meet me in this room for a reason, as you can see the wall behind me contains relics from the past. The wars and battles over a millennium, that has made our land the envy of the world.   We never give in, we fight, we win, and we bring the rewards back into our lives. The wall behind me speaks of valour in battle, and how a strong will and devotion to a common purpose can make us great. I have had thoughts about what you told me Boris, and this alien knowledge was offered only to one man. Not you, nor our great Federation. I have my doubts that you pair have bought anything that will come close to the rewards behind me. I live in hope, so show me what you have!'

Boris removed the egg from the box and held it out in his left hand. To the President it was nothing, it was just an egg of steel:

'What is this? A joke, what does it do:'

'It is the device that we know was receiving information from an alien source.'

'Is it working?'

'Yes, I believe so, but we may have to have our scientists study it.'

Boris continued to hold his left arm out straight, for some reason he thought holding it would trigger the response. The President was not amused, he now thought this whole exercise was a waste of time. However, just then the egg began to glow purple, with a strange jelly like appearance. A purple haze encompassed the egg and Boris's hand:

'It's getting quite warm I believe it is about to tell us something!'

The next few seconds were very traumatic. The egg suddenly went bright purple and dissolved, at the same time dissolving Boris's hand and cauterising the wound. He screamed in agony. All three men were in a state of shock, the two security guards ran over to assist. The Presidents initial shock became anger. He looked at the two agents with disgust, then with a wave of his hand beckoned the guards:

'Take these two idiots away! We have a place for foolish cripples, they can spend the rest of their lives in a Siberian Gulag for their stupidity in this whole exercise.'

The Oligarch Boris was no more, he was stripped of his wealth and his family plunged into poverty. Sadly, there would be no modern prosthetic for his missing hand. A steel make-shift hook would forever stand as a reminder to his folly.

CHAPTER NINETEEN

Fortress Tasmania

L ife settled back to normal after Arnolds return, the project was shut down pending a discussion on future developments. There was talk with the Premier, on establishing a new base on a State-owned Island, after returning Freycinet back to its original National Park status. All this will happen in time. Rachelle was given a promotion to run a D.O.N.T office in Hobart. With Arnold they then planned their marriage. A memorial to Peabody and Christian, was held at the Lodge. That was followed by a project completion celebration, that recognized the possible 'Wormhole' technological break-through, that Arnold reported. It was a great night of dancing, memories, and stories. Clarkey was seen dancing with Bream and romance was in the air.

As far as Covid-19 was concerned, Australia dodged

a bullet, for now. Immunisation acceptance was slow, but travel bubbles were opening. Life would never get back to normal. Eventually fortress Tasmania would be the saving grace. Rachelle and Arnold would build their dream home in the Hobart hinterland. Future flood proofing for their children.

Marlin was in his Hobart office on the 15 July 2024. It had been 72 years since he was given the alien egg. Today was his eightieth birthday. That night Bream was preparing a party for him at the Winery, and it was going to be a big occasion. Sally was there with him in the office, he was looking at Gaffers hook, it had found a new home here. He turned to Sally with a tear in his eye:

'I wonder what old Gaffer would have thought of our adventure Sal?'

'He would probably say, God works in mysterious ways.'

The only thing faster than the Covid-19's mutations were the number of deaths across the planet. In India four thousand or more people, were dying daily. The vaccines offered only a hiatus to stabilise the steady stream of burials. Third world countries fared the worst, whereas the rich countries, looked after their own people first. These mutations found ways around the effectiveness of all the diverse types of vaccines that were developed. Summers were getting hotter, food scarcer and societies in decline, just as predicted. In Tasmania, attitudes were changing under Premier Thompson. It was one of the very few places in the world that seemed to be on top of their game. Fortress Tasmania was about to be created, and the cull continued. In time, Marlin's daughter Sole, would be the Premier of the State.

Humans would survive and repopulate the planet, leaving vast swathes of wildlife parks, so nature could once again establish control. Eventually, there would be a new world order, based in a newly built Hobart, well above the predicted sea level rise. Science would become the new religion. The environment would slowly normalise, with a human population of less than a billion, living with the land not owning it.

The future possibilities for Marvin's prototypes were endless. The electro-gravitic model would create a new form of travel, possibly allowing connections to various parts of the known universe via Wormholes. Future travellers arriving through these portals, many light years from earth, would have instant communication via Marlin's Entangled Particle Morse. Time dilation effects would be minimalised by such instant transport, and only subject to the destinations gravity mass. The nano poly-bricks, with artificial intelligence and built-in blueprints, would replace supply lines for all the nano-electric devices.

Eventually humans could have access to the entire universe. They would find basic life on many worlds. Earth like water planets, in the Goldilocks Zones of far-off Solar Systems, would be sourced and where possible colonised. Finding alien intelligent life would be the goal of future Obernauts. Humans would continue to discover, evolve, and eventually find purpose in existence. At least for an appropriate time in an infinite universe. None of this would have been possible without the MUZE intervention.

The MUZE would forever look on, convinced that their interference was necessary, because they believed they had found their creators.

———

ABOUT THE AUTHOR

Gary John Carter

I was born in July 1952 in Western Sydney, a lucky time to be alive. I worked in the Electrical supply industry. I have lived a basic suburban life and avoided the stepping-stones of strife. I planted a few trees as my houses turned to homes. I had a son and a daughter, and I am also blessed with grandchildren. I love to tell stories and now I have authored some books.

Now that my days are now running faster I am grateful for the cause and effect granted by the 'Big Bangs' master.

BOOKS BY THIS AUTHOR

Where Eels Lie Down

This is a colloquial yarn with a 'boys own' twist that crosses the river of time. The settings are a lake reserve, a local pub, and the streets of Parramatta. They blend history, local issues, and 'Dreamtime' mysticism. This is all mixed in with the life and love of a man and woman, whose feelings are woven by nature, at the place where the eels lie down.

ISBN: 978-0-9953680-4-0

About That Shout

The history of Pubs, Inns and Hostelries in Parramatta. The book contains an account of past and present hotels and inns of Parramatta, and some of the stories within, dating from 1800 to the present.

ISBN: 978-0-9953680-1-9